AND BABY MAKES THREE

"You're not serious," Kelly said, stunned.

Jordan revealed a stunning diamond engagement ring that proclaimed him to be dead serious.

"I've given it a lot of thought. We've known each other forever, and I can give you the kind of life you deserve," he said.

"And I can give you...what? A bed partner on cold nights?"

Jordan could feel the blood climbing into his cheeks. That thought had occurred to him. "Now, Kelly—"

"Not a chance."

But Kelly doubted she could hold out against his ludicrous proposal for very long. She'd been in love with the man practically since the cradle.

Trouble was, he wasn't in love with her....

AND BABY MAKES THREE:
The Adams men of Texas all find love—and fatherhood—in most unexpected ways!

Dear Reader,

Silhouette Special Edition welcomes you to a new year filled with romance! Our Celebration 1000! continues in 1996, and where better to begin the new year than with Debbie Macomber's *Just Married*. Marriage and a baby await a mercenary in the latest tale from this bestselling author.

Next we have our HOLIDAY ELOPEMENTS title for the month, Lisa Jackson's *New Year's Daddy*, where a widowed single mom and a single dad benefit from a little matchmaking. Concluding this month is MORGAN'S MERCENARIES: LOVE AND DANGER. Lindsay McKenna brings her newest series to a close with *Morgan's Marriage*.

But wait, there's more—other favorites making an appearance in January include *Cody's Fiancée*, the latest in THE FAMILY WAY series from Gina Ferris Wilkins. And Sherryl Woods's book, *Natural Born Daddy*, is part of her brand-new series called AND BABY MAKES THREE, about the Adams men of Texas. Finally this month, don't miss a wonderful opposites-attract story from Susan Mallery, *The Bodyguard & Ms. Jones*.

Hope this New Year shapes up to be the best year ever! Enjoy this book and all the books to come!

Sincerely,

Tara Gavin
Senior Editor

Please address questions and book requests to:
Silhouette Reader Service
U.S.: 3010 Walden Ave., P.O. Box 1325, Buffalo, NY 14269
Canadian: P.O. Box 609, Fort Erie, Ont. L2A 5X3

SHERRYL WOODS

NATURAL BORN DADDY

Silhouette®

SPECIAL EDITION®

Published by Silhouette Books
America's Publisher of Contemporary Romance

SILHOUETTE BOOKS

ISBN 0-373-24007-4

NATURAL BORN DADDY

Copyright © 1996 by Sherryl Woods

This edition published by arrangement with Harlequin Books S.A.

® and TM are trademarks of Harlequin Books S.A., used under license. Trademarks indicated with ® are registered in the United States Patent and Trademark Office, the Canadian Trade Marks Office and in other countries.

Printed in U.S.A.

Books by Sherryl Woods

SHERRYL WOODS

lives by the ocean, which, she says, provides daily inspiration for the romance in her soul. She further explains that her years as a television critic taught her about steamy plots and humor; her years as a travel editor took her to exotic locations; and her years as a crummy weekend tennis player taught her to stick with what she enjoyed most—writing. "What better way is there," Sherryl asks, "to combine all that experience than by creating romantic stories?" Sherryl loves to hear from her readers. You may write to her at P.O. Box 490326, Key Biscayne, FL 33149. A self-addressed, stamped envelope is appreciated for a reply.

OUR FAMILY
Baby
ME
Daddy
Mommy
Jordan
CAT
DRAWING by Dani ADAMS

Prologue

"Hey, boss, the barracuda... excuse me, your fiancée is on line two," Ginger Drake announced from the doorway.

Jordan glowered at his impudent secretary. "I've told you not to call her that."

Undaunted, Ginger merely strolled into his office and perched on the corner of his desk, an act that hiked her skirt to midthigh. Jordan shook his head. If she weren't the most efficient, most incredibly loyal young woman who'd ever worked for him, he would have fired her months ago for her tart remarks and her unrepentant intrusion into his personal life.

"You've also told me to be honest and truthful, no matter how much it hurts," she informed him now. "That's my job around here."

"Your job is taking dictation and typing."

"And keeping you happy," she reminded him. She gestured at the blinking phone line. "*She* does not make you happy. She is a b—"

"Don't say it," he warned, reaching for the phone.

Ginger shrugged. "Well, she is, which you could see for yourself, if you weren't blinded by the size of her—"

"Ginger!" He pointed toward the door. "Out!"

"Just doing my job," she said, and sashayed from the room with a provocative sway of her hips.

Unable to resist, Jordan watched that motion with an appreciative eye. If he hadn't known that she was blissfully married to a linebacker for the Houston Oilers, he would have assumed that Ginger was trying to get his attention. Instead, he knew perfectly well that feminine provocation came as naturally and unselfconsciously to her as flirting with the opposite sex did to him. The difference was, he had tired of it.

Being named one of the city's most eligible bachelors the past five years in a row had lost its charm. He was ready to settle down. The woman on the phone was the candidate he'd chosen six months ago from the string of female acquaintances who accompanied him to the various charity functions that made up the bulk of his social life.

"Hey, darlin', how are you?" he said to Rexanne Marshall once Ginger was out of hearing range with the office door firmly shut behind her. "How was the convention?"

"Interesting," Rexanne said in that deliberately smoky voice that oozed sensuality and, as she well knew, sent goose bumps dancing down his spine.

He settled back in his chair and asked, "Did you make any big deals?" Rexanne really got turned on by her deal making. He could practically envision their passionate reunion.

"You could say that."

Jordan thought he heard something odd in her tone, a hint of strain that was rare for the supremely confident, highly successful owner of a small but thriving Texas cosmetics company. It was a company poised to make a major move into the national marketplace with his financial backing.

"Rexanne, is everything okay?"

"Jordan..."

He could hear her swallowing and suddenly his body went absolutely still. She had bad news. He could tell from that increasingly evident note of uncertainty in her voice. He sat up a little straighter.

"Whatever it is, just tell me," he instructed. He'd meant to sound patient and concerned, but even he recognized the drill-sergeant command in his voice.

"Actually, it was the most amazing thing," she began with a nervous little giggle.

Rexanne was quite possibly the most sophisticated woman he'd ever met. She never giggled. His suspicions tripled as he waited for her to go on.

"I ran into this man, an old friend, actually, from high school, as a matter of fact."

Now the woman who never wasted a word was babbling. Jordan's sense of dread kicked in. He stood and began to pace, phone in hand. "And?"

"Well, the truth of it is...Jordan, I'm really sorry about this, but..."

"Just spit it out, Rexanne."

"Randall and I got married," she blurted at last. "In Vegas."

Rexanne and Randall? How alliterative, he thought with an uncharacteristic edge of sarcasm. Married? How considerate of her to give him fair warning. The same society page columnists who'd been gushing about their engagement would be gossiping about this turn of events for weeks. It was only one step short of being left at the altar. He didn't like the prospect of being the subject of speculation and innuendo. He didn't like it one damned bit.

"I see," he said coldly. Not entirely sure of the protocol for the circumstances, he went with his gut reaction, which was liberally laced with more sarcasm. "Thank you so much for calling, Rexanne. Have a nice life."

"Now, Jordan, please don't be like that," she whined.

Why had he never noticed that she whined? he wondered. Probably because he'd given in to her every request, showered her with gifts and never once in the months since they had announced their engagement exchanged a cross word with her. Of course, that was probably because Rexanne had tucked herself so neatly and cheerfully into his life, he'd had no reason to complain.

"Darling, I know it's a shock and I wouldn't have hurt you for the world, but this was, like, fate or something," she said in a more familiar, smoky, cajoling tone.

"Fate?" he repeated numbly. "Yes, I suppose it was." *Fate* had benevolently prevented him from having to listen to that whine for the rest of his days. She could ooze sensuality from now to doomsday and he would never stop hearing that whine. It would lurk in his memory like the sound of chalk squeaking across a blackboard.

"Darling, you can't let this change in our personal status interfere with the business arrangement we have," she protested. "You're too much of a businessman. You and I are going to take Marshall Cosmetics to the top around the globe. We're going to make a fortune."

Ah, now they were getting to her real concern, not his feelings, but her future plans for Marshall Cosmetics. "Sorry, *darlin'*, I'm afraid that's going to be up to you and Randall."

"But you promised," she whined.

The sound of her voice was really getting on his nerves. "So did you," he reminded her icily. "Goodbye, Rexanne."

He hung up before she could launch into an attempt to sugarcoat the now-obvious truth—that she had wanted his money and his connections to Wall Street more than she had ever wanted him.

As he sat staring out at the sweeping view of the Houston skyline, he wondered at his lack of emotion. Shouldn't he have felt more than this vague irritation that his plans for settling down had been disrupted? Shouldn't he be feeling empty inside? Shouldn't he be throwing things? He hefted a Baccarat crystal paperweight consideringly, then shrugged and lowered it to his desk. She wasn't worth it.

Maybe he was incapable of the kind of passion that his older brother Luke had found with Jessie. Maybe, he conceded, he'd gone about finding a wife too methodically.

Or maybe the incredible judgment that had propelled him to the top of the oil industry didn't carry over into personal matters. Maybe he was doomed to make the same mistakes over and over, trusting the wrong women.

It wasn't, he admitted to himself ruefully, as if Rexanne had been the first. There had been a whole damned army of poor choices, starting back in college and continuing right up through this latest debacle. Oddly enough, he realized he couldn't even recall the names of most of them. Obviously his heart had never been as engaged as he'd thought it had been.

Finally, dragging in a deep breath, he pushed the problem aside for further consideration on the weekend. He was almost tempted to make a notation to himself on his calendar, so he wouldn't forget. *Women* ought to be enough of a reminder. He reached for his daybook and dutifully jotted it down. He would matter-of-factly dissect his love life as he would a business proposition to see if he could pinpoint where he was going wrong.

He turned back to his desk just in time to see Ginger poking her head into his office. The grin on her face made him wonder if she'd been eavesdropping on his conversation. She'd apparently seen all along what he hadn't, that Rexanne was a barracuda. No doubt that smile meant she was delighted that the woman was out of his life.

"Hey, boss, didn't you hear me buzzing you?" she asked.

"If I had, I would have answered," he retorted irritably.

Her grin widened. She knew, all right, he decided with a sinking feeling. It appeared his latest humiliation was complete. There would be weeks of hearing *I told you so* from her, interspersed with renewed attempts at matchmaking. Maybe he'd finally give in. Ginger's taste couldn't possibly be any worse than his own, though she did seem to know a disturbing number of professional cheerleaders.

"Line one," she prompted him. "It's Kelly."

For some inexplicable reason, Jordan found himself smiling back at his secretary. If there was one person on the face of the earth who could take his mind off his troubles, it was Kelly Flint. She was his best friend, his confidante, his conscience. She had an angel of mercy's sense of timing .

As he reached for the phone the most incredible thought flashed through his head. Why the devil couldn't he marry a woman like Kelly? She was sweet, not the least bit temperamental, funny and, though he'd never really stopped to think about it before—at least not since the days when they'd gone swimming in the creek together back in west Texas—sexy. In fact, just thinking about her sex appeal made him wonder why he hadn't settled on Kelly as the perfect solution long ago.

"Why, indeed?" he murmured thoughtfully, picturing her in his head and liking what he saw—clean-scrubbed, basic beauty with absolutely no artifice about her. Better yet, he knew for a fact that she didn't have a duplicitous bone in her body. She would never betray the man she loved.

"What was that, boss?" Ginger asked, regarding him with a puzzled look.

"Nothing," he said, because confiding in Ginger would only draw more advice than he could handle right now. "Nothing at all."

Something told him, though, that the disclaimer was more than a massive understatement. He had a feeling he had just reached the most significant turning point in his entire life. He mentally scratched the subject of women from his calendar and replaced it with one word: *Kelly*.

By the end of the day he would have his plan for marrying her formulated and by the weekend he'd be ready to put it into action. Unless something unforeseen popped up, he and Kelly could be married and settled down by fall. He wouldn't even have to alter the schedule he'd set for himself when he'd asked Rexanne to marry him.

Pleased with himself, he finally poked the blinking light on his phone. "Hey, darlin'," he said, taking what he perceived to be the first step on the road to the rest of his life.

Chapter One

Jordan drove up the dusty, shaded lane to Kelly's ranch in west Texas with a rare knot in his stomach. Once he'd gotten the idea of marrying her into his head, he hadn't been able to shake it loose. It had been like a burr, sticking to him and snagging his attention at the oddest times.

The only thing that had prevented him from impulsively proposing to her on the phone when she'd called his office earlier in the week was Ginger's fascinated expression as she stood beside his desk the whole time he was on the phone. He had a gut-level feeling that even though his secretary might have applauded Rexanne's replacement, there was something vaguely tacky about proposing to a woman not five minutes after being dumped by the previous fiancée.

Over the next few days the previously implausible idea of marrying his best friend had begun to take shape in his head. He could actually envision Kelly at his side for the rest of his life.

As he'd reminded himself when the idea first came to him, she was calm, sweet and beautiful, at least when she wasn't covered head-to-toe in filth from a rough day on the range. Of course, that wouldn't be a problem once they were married and she was living with him in Houston. She'd have endless hours to pamper herself.

With her glowing skin, her hair the color of wheat in sunlight, and her unexpected brown eyes, she would knock the socks off of Houston society. With her warmth, she would be an asset as a hostess for the kinds of functions that were required of a corporate president. His friends and associates would find her tales of running her own ranch intriguing, if something of an oddity for a woman alone.

Well, not alone, exactly, he reminded himself. There was Danielle. The preschooler was the by-product of Kelly's unfortunate marriage to Paul Flint, a philanderer of the first order, a man who had taken Kelly's tender, trusting heart and broken it into pieces.

Hands clenched and temper barely contained, Jordan had witnessed most of that particular debacle. He'd provided the shoulder for Kelly to cry on when she'd finally decided to end the marriage and take her daughter home to Los Pinos, the tiny west Texas town where they'd grown up on neighboring ranches.

Danielle was a bit of a complication, he had to admit. He was lousy with kids. He had no idea what to say to them. In all of his plans for settling down, he rarely considered the next step—kids.

He thought back to the previous Christmas. When his sister-in-law had shown up at the family ranch with his infant niece, he'd been completely stymied about what to do with that fragile little baby. Even the prospect of holding her had made his palms sweat. He'd tried not to let his reaction show, but he had known that he had negotiated multimillion-dollar business deals with less display of nerves.

Danielle was equally perplexing to him, even though in a fit of sentiment he'd allowed himself to be persuaded to be her godfather.

The child was barely three feet tall, he reminded himself. At five, she already had an astonishing and precocious vocabulary. Surely he could find a way to communicate with her. If nothing else, he could always buy her half the stock at Toys Unlimited. She'd be so busy with all those new playthings, she wouldn't require any attention at all from him.

Satisfied that he'd dealt with that potential problem in his usual decisive way, he drew in a deep breath and rehearsed what he would say to Kelly to persuade her to marry him. For all of his planning, this part had never quite solidified the way it should have. He kept envisioning her laughing in his face, amused by his out-of-the-blue proposal after all these years of platonic friendship.

Perhaps he should simply tell her that she was the answer to his prayers, someone he liked, someone he trusted.

Someone who could keep him out of the clutches of the wrong women. Even as the words formed, he groaned. Telling her that would certainly go a long way toward charming her. No matter how unemotional she might be, even a woman who'd been chosen as the solution to a problem of sorts wanted to be wooed a little. As a practical matter, he knew Kelly would see the sense of his proposal, but he would definitely have to dress it up with a little romance.

Damn, how was he going to pull this off? Kelly was the most fiercely independent woman he'd ever met, especially since her divorce. She might not want to marry anyone after her experience with Paul, especially not a man who, at one time or another, had been pictured on the society pages with half of Houston's eligible female population. His track record, though certainly not immoral, might be a too vivid reminder of her ex's habits.

Since the divorce, Kelly had taken charge of her life. She had returned to the falling down ranch her family had left her and tackled the task of making it work with the kind of gritty determination he couldn't help but admire.

For the past two years she had worn herself ragged, working from before dawn until well after dark, seven days a week. The ranch hardly had a look of prosperity about it, but there was no mistaking that her efforts were paying off. There was fresh paint on the old house, inside and out, and her herd of longhorns was growing. Even now the livestock was visible in the distance, grazing on newly acquired pastureland she had bought with every penny of her divorce settlement.

The hard work should have taken its toll, but, he was forced to admit, in recent months Kelly had never looked healthier or happier. She no longer had the haggard, tight-lipped, stricken look of a woman who'd been betrayed by the man she'd loved. In fact, she glowed, radiating a sense of serenity and bone-deep satisfaction that had made visiting her the highlight of his trips home.

Whenever the weighty sense of family that Harlan Adams imposed on all of his sons grew too burdensome, Jordan slipped away from White Pines and spent time in Kelly's kitchen, sipping the herbal tea she preferred and talking of inconsequential things that somehow all added up to a kind of tranquillity he found nowhere else in his life. The thought of spending the rest of his days around a woman capable of creating such a peaceful atmosphere soothed him.

Okay, so they wouldn't be marrying for love. Neither of them had had much luck with messy emotions anyway. An old-style marriage of convenience struck him as the sensible way to go. Kelly would never have to worry about money for herself or her daughter again and he would never have to deal with another female barracuda.

As he walked toward the front porch of the ranch house, a porch that sagged and dipped from years of use and sloppy construction, he noted the huge pots of bright flowers she tended with such care in the evenings. They were thriving, the blossoms providing vivid splashes of color against the front of the white house.

Already anticipating their life together, he sighed with contentment. Kelly was a nurturer. Like those flowers, he and any children they ultimately might have would thrive in her care. Assuming he got over this uneasiness he felt with these pint-size enigmas, that is.

He fingered the small jewelry box in his pocket and smiled, pleased with his decision. Kelly's fat gray-and-white cat wound between his legs, purring and shedding on his navy pants. Jordan glanced down, felt a momentary touch of annoyance, then sighed. The old tomcat was part of the package and at least he seemed delighted by Jordan's presence.

With a rare twinge of trepidation, he knocked on the screen door and called out, "Hey, darlin', it's me."

He heard the thunder of tiny feet as Dani came careering around a corner and raced down the hallway. She skidded to a halt, her blond curls bouncing.

"Hi, Jordan," she said, swinging the screen door wide and coming out to join him. "Mommy's in the barn. Francie's having kittens. A lot of kittens."

Jordan cringed. "Really?"

"Want to come see?"

He would rather eat dirt, but the sparkle of anticipation in Dani's eyes was too powerful to resist. "Sure."

To his astonishment, Dani tucked her hand trustingly in his and tugged him around the side of the house toward the barn. "You could have one, if you wanted," she told him.

"I work very long hours. I'm not sure what I'd do with a kitten in Houston," he said, trying to sound as if he regretted it when the truth was he couldn't have been more relieved.

"Cats don't mind if you're not home very much. They're very independent," she informed him. "We hardly ever see Francie, except when she's going to have kittens."

Old Francie reminded him of certain types of people who only turned up when they were in trouble. He hoped Kelly wasn't going to view his visit that way.

Dani stopped on the path in front of him, her face turned up, her brow knitted with concern. "Mommy says we have to give all of them away," she told him.

Her eyes suddenly and, Jordan thought, rather suspiciously filled with tears.

"What if we can't find homes for them?" she asked, sounding pathetic. "Will we have to drown them in the creek?"

The little minx was pulling out all the stops. Jordan choked back a chuckle at the preposterous notion that Kelly would allow harm to come to a single kitten. "No, Dani, I seriously doubt that your mother would drown them in the creek. Where would you ever get such an idea?"

"That's what Daddy said should happen to kittens."

"But you didn't do it, did you?"

"No, because I found homes for every single one." She looked up at him speculatively. "Maybe they'd like a new kitten at White Pines. I'll bet there are mice there and everything. A kitten would be a big help."

"I'll ask," he told her, wondering what his mother would have to say about a kitten scratching her precious antique furniture.

"Promise?"

"Cross my heart."

A radiant smile spread across her face. "Thanks, Jordan. I really, really think you should take one, too. So you won't be lonely."

Actually, he had another idea for staving off loneliness. He glanced up and saw the very woman he had in mind standing in the barn, hands on slender hips, a challenging spark in her eyes as she regarded her daughter.

"You have your work cut out for you, young lady," Kelly announced, barely sparing a glance for Jordan. "There are seven kittens in here. Francie's tuckered out and so am I. See to it that Francie has some fresh food and water."

"Cream, Mommy. Don't you think she deserves cream just this once? Having kittens is hard work."

"Fine, bring her some cream."

Dani tore off across the lawn as fast as her churning little legs could carry her.

"And don't put it in a good china bowl! Use plastic," Kelly shouted after her. Finally she glanced at Jordan. "What brings you by on a Friday night? You didn't mention anything about coming home when we talked earlier in the week."

Jordan shrugged. He was struck by an uncharacteristic twinge of uncertainty. He tucked his hand into his pocket and tightened his grip around the jewelry box for reassurance. "Just an impulse."

"Come on in. I'll make us some tea. Chamomile, I think. You look almost as frazzled as I feel."

"You don't look frazzled," he noted even though it was a charitable remark. Her hair was tousled, her makeup nonexistent, her clothes caked with mud and hay and other stains that didn't bear too close a scrutiny.

Inside the cozy kitchen, which was shadowed in the gathering twilight, she smiled at him. She took down two china cups and placed them on the kitchen table. "And you're a lousy liar, despite all that practice you get dispensing your charm all over Houston. How's the oil business?"

"Challenging."

Attuned as always to his moods, she paused while filling the teakettle with water. "Bad week?"

"No worse than most."

Her gaze narrowed. "That doesn't sound convincing, old chum."

Jordan picked up the empty cup and turned it slowly in his hands. The fine porcelain was cracked and chipped, but he found the delicacy oddly enchanting. Flaws, he'd discovered over time, often made people, like china, more interesting. He wondered what flaws Kelly had. After all these years, he could think of none. Discovering them suddenly struck him as a fascinating pastime.

"Jordan?"

He looked up from the fragile cup and saw that Kelly was regarding him with a puzzled expression.

Those huge brown eyes of hers were filled with concern.

"Everything okay?" she asked.

"Rexanne broke the engagement," he announced casually.

"Good," Kelly replied without the slightest hint of sympathy.

"Damn," he muttered irritably. "Did everybody dislike her except me?"

"I didn't dislike her," Kelly corrected. "I just thought she was all wrong for you."

"Why?"

"She was using you."

"Weren't they all," he said dryly.

"As a matter of fact, yes," she said as she poured the boiling water into the pot, tossed in a handful of tea leaves and waited for it to steep.

"Have you ever approved of any woman I've dated?"

Kelly took the question he'd intended to be sarcastic seriously. "There was one, back in college. I think her name was Pamela. You dumped her after the first date."

"And she was right for me?"

"I didn't have all that long to check out her sincerity," she reminded him, "but, yes, I think she could have been. She was sweet."

Jordan scowled. *Sweet?* Perhaps innocuous would have been a better description. He didn't even remember a Pamela, which didn't say much for either her or him.

"Actually, I think my taste is improving," he said, his gaze fixed on Kelly's face. There was no immediate reaction beyond a faint flicker of something in her eyes, something he couldn't quite identify. She seemed slightly more alert, perhaps even a little wary.

"You've already found a replacement for Rexanne? Isn't that a little cavalier?"

"Not really. I told you a long time ago that I thought it was time for me to settle down."

"Right, so you proposed to the first woman to cross your path after that, and look where that got you."

"She wasn't the first woman to cross my path," he protested. "I was seeing several women at the time. Rexanne seemed like the best choice."

"Maybe out of that lot, but did you ever stop to consider there was slim pickings in that bunch?" She waggled a slender finger at him. "I'll answer that. No, you did not. You just decided you wanted to be married and filled the opening as methodically as you would have a position at your company. You probably had a stupid checksheet."

She wasn't all that far off the mark, though he wouldn't have told her that for another gusher in his oil fields. "Well, I'm not going to be so hasty about it this time," he said.

"You just told me you've identified the woman you want to marry. It's been what? Two days? Maybe three since your engagement broke off?"

"Four, actually."

She rolled her eyes. "Definitely long enough," she said with a touch of unfamiliar sarcasm. "Jordan, why can't you just relax and let nature take its course?''

He gave her a disdainful look. "I don't have a lot of faith in nature."

She gave him a wry look. "You would if you'd been in that barn with me an hour ago."

"I don't think the fact that your tomcat can't keep his paws off of Francie is a testament to nature in its finest moments."

She shrugged, a grin tugging at the corners of her mouth. "Okay, you may have a point about that. So, who's the latest woman to capture your fancy?"

He leveled a look straight into her eyes and waited until he was sure he had her full attention. "Actually, it's you."

Kelly—calm, serene, unflappable Kelly—succumbed to a coughing fit that had her eyes watering and Jordan wondering if he'd gone about this in an incredibly stupid way. It wouldn't be the first time the direct method had failed him.

Still, he was determined to make her see the sense of this. All of those lectures he'd given himself about dressing it up with a little sweet talk flew out the window. He set out to hammer home the logic.

"It's a perfectly rational decision . . ." he began.

"You're not serious," she said when she could finally speak.

He pulled the jewelry box from his pocket and placed it on the kitchen table in front of her. Since she was eyeing it as if it were a poisonous rattler, he flipped it open to reveal a stunning three-carat diamond that pretty well proclaimed him to be dead serious. Despite its impressive size, it was simpler than the engagement ring he'd purchased at Rexanne's urging. She'd wanted flashy. Kelly struck him as the kind of woman who would admire simplicity. Gazing into her eyes, however, he had the sinking feeling that admiration for his taste in rings was the last thing on her mind.

"You've obviously lost your mind," she said, but her voice was softer now and laced with something that might have been regret.

"Quite the contrary. It's the only rational decision for both of us."

"Rational," she repeated as if it were a dirty word.

There was an ominous undercurrent he didn't quite get. "Actually, yes. I've given it quite a lot of thought. We've known each other forever—there won't be any nasty surprises. We've both had more than our share of those. I can give you the kind of life and financial security you deserve."

"And I can give you... what? A hostess? A cook, perhaps? A bed partner on cold nights?"

Jordan could feel the blood climbing into his cheeks as she enumerated some of the very thoughts that had occurred to him. They'd sounded better in theory than they did spoken out loud by a woman who was clearly insulted. She wasn't taking this well at all. He searched for a new approach. "Now, Kelly..."

Unfortunately he never got to finish the sentence. Kelly was already shaking her head, rather emphatically, it seemed to him.

She stood and glowered down at him. "Not a chance. No way. Forget it, bud. Take a hike." She seemed to be just warming up.

The flare of unexpected temper just might be one of those previously hidden flaws he'd been hoping to discover. He tried to calm her. "You're saying no without giving the matter any consideration at all," he advised her. "When you do, I'm sure you'll see—"

"Not if we both live to be a hundred and ten and we're the only two people tottering around on the face of the earth," she assured him.

Jordan was beginning to get an inkling that she meant it and that nothing he was likely to say tonight was going to change her mind.

"Okay, okay," he said, defeated for the moment. "I get the picture."

"I doubt it."

A hasty exit seemed in order. "Maybe I'd better let you sleep on it. We can talk again tomorrow."

Kelly drew herself up and squared off in front of him. Fire sparked in her eyes, amber lights bringing that normally placid shade of brown alive. "We can talk tomorrow, if you like," she said emphatically, "but not about this."

Jordan edged carefully around her and made his way to the front door. "See you in the morning."

"Jordan?"

Her voice halted him in his tracks. She had obviously followed him.

"You forgot something."

He turned back. She was holding out the box with the engagement ring. "Keep it here," he said, refusing to accept it. "Try it on. Maybe you'll get used to the idea."

She tossed the ring straight at him. He caught it in midair and sighed. "I'll bring it with me tomorrow."

"Don't," she warned angrily. "I'm not some poor substitute you can call on when the first string doesn't show."

Jordan was shocked by her assessment, even though he had to admit there might be just the teensiest bit of truth to it. "I'm sorry. I never meant it like that," he insisted.

She sighed heavily. "Yes, Jordan, I think that is exactly how you meant it."

That said, she quietly closed the door in his face. He was left standing on the porch all alone. Oddly enough, it was the first time in all the visits he had paid to this house that he was leaving feeling lonelier and far, far emptier than when he had arrived.

He made up his mind as he drove the few miles back to White Pines that night that that wouldn't be the last of it. After all, hadn't he wooed some of the most sought-after women in all of Texas? Maybe approaching this as a business proposition hadn't been the wisest decision. He'd try roses and, if that didn't work, billboards along the highway, if he had to. Nobody said no to Jordan Adams. Kelly would weaken sooner or later. What struck him as slightly worrisome was the fact that it suddenly seemed to matter so much. Somewhere deep inside him he had the troubling impression that she was his last and best chance for happiness.

"The man is impossible!" Kelly declared, leaning against the front door and listening for the sound of his car driving off before she budged. She didn't want to move until she knew for certain he wasn't coming back. She seriously doubted she could hold out against his ludicrous proposal for very long. She'd been in love with the man practically since the cradle.

Unfortunately he had never once in all these years given her a second glance. She doubted he would be doing it now, if he hadn't suffered a defeat in his blasted plan for his own life. Who in hell had a timetable for getting married? No one she knew except Jordan Adams. Well, he could put that plan into action without her.

"Mommy, are you okay?" Dani asked, peering up at her.

"I sure am, munchkin," she said with more exuberance than she felt.

"You look funny."

She grinned at the honest assessment. Bending over, she scooped her daughter into her arms and swung her high. "Funny?" she repeated indignantly. "Mommy is beautiful, remember?"

Dani giggled from her upside-down vantage point. "Very beautiful," she confirmed. "Let me down, Mommy. My head's getting dizzy."

"Mine, too, sweetie," she murmured, glancing through the window and watching the red glow of Jordan's taillights disappear into the night.

Suddenly she thought of all the times she'd watched Jordan drive away, her heart thudding with disappointment once more because he hadn't recognized how perfect they were for each other, because his kiss had been nothing more than a peck on the cheek.

She'd married Paul Flint only after she'd finally faced up to the fact that Jordan was never going to view her as anything more than his pal. Her world had fallen apart after that stupid, impulsive decision. Not right away, of course. It had taken a month or two before Paul had started spending more and more time away from their home. She wasn't even certain when he'd started seeing other women.

When she finally accepted the fact that Paul was having affairs, she asked for a divorce. Jordan had been there to pick up the pieces. He hadn't even said he'd told her so as he'd transported her and then three-year-old Dani to the ranch where Kelly had grown up.

From that moment on they had fallen into their old pattern of frequent phone calls and visits whenever he came home from Houston. She looked forward to their talks more and more. She had dreaded the day when his marriage to Rexanne would force an end to the quiet, uncomplicated time they spent together. ·

At least that wasn't a problem any longer, she thought with another sigh.

"Mommy? Are you sad?" Dani inquired with her astonishing perceptiveness.

"Just a little," she admitted.

"I know just what you need," her daughter announced, giving her a coy look that Kelly recognized all too well.

"What's that?"

"A new kitten."

Kelly grinned at her child's sneaky tactics. The suggestion was certainly a more rational one than Jordan had offered. A kitten was a whole lot less complicated than taking on a husband who'd selected her for marriage for all the wrong reasons.

"I'll think about it," she promised. "Now, go take your bath and get ready for bed."

Dani bounced off toward the stairs, then halted and looked back. "Mommy?"

"Yes."

"Think really hard, okay?"

"Okay."

It was the second time that night that she'd been asked to carefully consider a decision that could change her life. Instinct told her to say no to both requests. Her heart was another matter entirely.

Chapter Two

Jordan lingered over coffee at White Pines the morning after his proposal to Kelly. He'd been up since the crack of dawn, in the dining room since six-thirty. All that time he'd been pondering a new approach to the problem of getting Kelly to take his declaration of his intentions seriously. For the first time in his life, he was at a loss.

He heard the sound of boots on the stairs and glanced toward the doorway. Harlan Adams appeared a moment later, looking as fit as ever despite the fact that his fifty-sixth birthday was just around the corner. He regarded his son with surprise. Jordan suspected it was feigned, since nothing went on around White Pines that his father didn't know within minutes.

"Hey, boy, when did you turn up?" his father asked as he surveyed the lavish breakfast buffet their housekeeper had left for them.

"Last night."

"Must have been mighty late."

"I'm too old for you to be checking my comings and goings," Jordan reminded his father.

"Did I ask?"

Jordan sighed and battled his instinctive reaction to his father's habitual, if subtle, probing. Harlan loved to goad them all, loved the spirited arguments and loved even more the rare wins he managed against his sons' stubbornness.

According to Luke, the oldest, their father battled wits with them just to get them to stand up for what they wanted. Jordan supposed it might be true. He'd practically had to declare war to leave White Pines and its ready-made career in ranching to go into the oil business. Yet once he'd gotten to Houston, the path had miraculously been cleared for him. He'd promptly found work at one of the best companies in the state before striking out on his own a few years later.

"Everything okay around here?" he inquired as his father piled his plate high with the scrambled eggs, ham and hash browns that were forbidden to him except on weekends. He noted with some amusement that Harlan gave wide berth to the bran flakes and oatmeal.

"Things would be just fine if Cody didn't decide he has to have some newfangled piece of equipment every time I turn around," Harlan grumbled.

"How many have you let him buy?" Jordan asked.

His father shrugged. "Put my foot down about some fancy computer with those little disks and intergalactic communications potential or some such. I can't even figure out the one we've got. Luke spent a whole day trying to show me again the last time he and Jessie were over here, but if you ask me, pen and paper are plenty good enough for keeping the books."

Jordan hid a smile. He knew that his father's pretended bemusement covered a mind that could grasp the most intricate details in a flash. Any trouble he was having with his computer was feigned solely to grab Luke's attention.

"Daddy, you're practically in the twenty-first century," he chided. "You have to keep up with the times."

"A lot of nonsense, if you ask me." He grinned. "Leastways, that's what I tell Cody. Keeps him on his toes."

The youngest of the Adams brothers, Cody was the one who'd fought hardest for his place as the head of the White Pines ranching operation. Harlan had pushed just as hard to get him to leave and strike out on his own. Now there was little question in anyone's mind that Cody was as integral to the family business as his father was.

"One of these days the two of you are going to butt heads once too often," Jordan warned his father.

"Not a chance," Harlan said with evident pride. "That boy's stubborn as a mule. Might even be worse than you or Lucas and he's a danged sight ornerier than Erik."

He sounded downright happy about his youngest's muleheadedness. He studied Jordan over the rim of his coffee cup. "You never did say what brought you home."

"No," Jordan said firmly. "I didn't."

"Wouldn't have anything to do with that Flint woman, would it?"

Jordan's head snapped up and he stared at his father. "Why would you ask that?"

"Because you make a beeline for that ranch every time you drive into the county. Can't be sleeping with her, since you do wind up in your own bed here at night."

Jordan's jaw tightened at the too personal observation. "My sleeping arrangements are none of your concern. Besides, Kelly and I are just friends. She's had a rough time of it these past couple of years. I try to look in on her every once in a while to make sure she's okay." At least, that had been his motivation until last night's visit.

His father nodded. "She's getting that place of hers on its feet, though. She's got a lot of gumption and that girl of hers is a real little dickens. She called here last night to see if you'd asked yet about whether we want a kitten."

Despite his annoyance with his father, Jordan couldn't help chuckling at Dani's persistence. The remark was also proof that his father had known he was back in town and had also known exactly where he was the night before. All the questions had been designed just to needle him.

"Did you agree to take one?" he asked, referring to the kittens Dani hadn't trusted him to save.

"How could I say no? The child was worried sick about her mother drowning them all in the creek. She mentioned that you'd reassured her that wouldn't happen, but she wasn't taking any chances." He eyed Jordan speculatively. "Does that pitiful excuse for a father of hers get by much?"

Jordan wasn't surprised that his father knew the whole ugly story. It was hardly a secret, but even if it had been, Harlan made it his business to know about the folks around him, including those on neighboring ranches. He was even more persistent when it came to the women in his sons' lives.

"Not that I'm aware of," he told his father.

"Can't understand a man who wouldn't be proud to call a little one like that his own."

"Neither can I," Jordan said grimly. He'd expressed his views on Paul Flint more than once to Kelly, long before she'd finally decided on divorce as her only option. He'd even offered on occasion to pummel some sense into the man.

"Shame to go through life without a daddy," Harlan observed.

Jordan regarded him intently. There was no mistaking that his father had a point to make. "Meaning?"

"Just what I said," he insisted, sounding a little too innocent. "A child deserves two parents. Of course, a situation like that is all wrong for a man like you."

"Now what's your point?" Jordan's voice contained a lethal warning note.

"Just that I understand you. You're not looking for some country gal and a ready-made family. I've seen your type, glossy, sophisticated, like that... what's her name?"

"Rexanne," Jordan supplied automatically, used to his father's refusal to get the names of the women in his life straight.

"Right," he said. "Now she's the perfect wife for a big oil tycoon."

Jordan was beginning to wonder exactly how much his father knew about his broken engagement. It seemed to him that the digs were a little too pointed for him not to have heard about it. He'd always despised Rexanne, just as he had every other woman Jordan had brought to White Pines. His sudden defense of her was clearly part of some Machiavellian scheme of his. He'd probably been on the phone to Ginger during the week and gotten an earful about his son's social life—or sudden lack thereof.

"I'm afraid Rexanne is out of the picture," Jordan said tersely.

Harlan tried for a sympathetic look, but the effort was downright pitiful. There was a gleam of pure satisfaction in his eyes. "Sorry, son," he said without much sincerity.

"She was the wrong choice. I'll get over it." Sooner than anyone imagined, if he had his way about it.

"It's not surprising, then, that you were over to visit Kelly last night. She always has had a sympathetic ear, especially where you're concerned."

"We weren't lamenting my love life last night," Jordan said.

Curiosity blossomed on his father's transparent features. "Oh?"

"We were just...talking," he finally concluded weakly, unwilling to broach the actual subject matter of their conversation. Once Harlan got that particular bit in his teeth, there'd be no controlling his efforts at manipulation.

"Just don't go letting her get the wrong idea now, son. You said yourself, she's been through a lot. No point in getting her hopes up now that you're on the rebound. No telling what a woman might do when a man is vulnerable. They can be downright sneaky when they're out to get their hooks into a man."

"There's nothing the least bit sneaky or underhanded about Kelly," Jordan snapped.

"If you say so, son. You certainly know the woman better than I do."

Jordan didn't think he liked the direction this conversation was heading. Any minute now his father was going to say something truly offensive about Kelly and he would leap to her defense. There was no telling what would happen after that. His mother would probably find them tussling on the dining room floor.

He tossed his napkin down on the table and stood. "I've got to get out of here."

"Going for a ride?" his father inquired, his expression perfectly innocent.

"Yes," he said tightly, and slammed out of the house.

Only much, much later did he wonder what he would have seen if he'd looked back. He had the strangest feeling he would have caught a complacent smile spreading across his father's face.

With Dani visiting a friend for the day, Kelly had spent the entire morning checking on her livestock and inspecting her fences. Of course, given her state of distraction an entire section of fence could have been down and it would have slipped her notice. Fortunately the ranch hand she'd been able to afford just a month ago had been riding with her most of the day. Now, though, she was alone again, riding at a more leisurely pace.

She kept glancing toward the horizon, looking for some sign of Jordan's car. Her ears were attuned to the sound of approaching hooves, as well, since he sometimes chose to borrow one of his father's horses and ride over.

He still looked incredibly well suited to horse and saddle. In fact, she'd always thought he looked far more impressive and a hundred percent sexier in jeans and a chambray shirt than he did in those outrageously expensive designer suits he wore most of the time in Houston. Every time he put one of those suits on, it was as if a barrier went up between them. Sometimes she didn't even recognize the man he'd become in Houston.

More than his clothes had changed. As if fitting himself to a role, he'd been transformed into a sophisticated executive, driven and sometimes, it seemed to her, a little too coldly dispassionate.

His proposal the night before had certainly fit the new Jordan. The old Jordan, the sensitive man who often sat in her kitchen talking until dawn, the exuberant daredevil who'd ridden over every square inch of her ranch and his own with her at midnight, would never have made such a proposition. He'd had more romance in his soul, even if little of it had been directed her way. Now she had to wonder if he'd wasted it all on that string of unsuitable gold diggers who'd spent the past few years trying to catch him.

She knew without a doubt that he wasn't going to give up on this crazy idea he'd gotten into his head about marrying her. One of his most attractive traits was his tenaciousness. To ready herself for the next assault, she had spent the entire morning reminding herself of all the ways to say no—and mean it.

She was so busy concentrating on shoring up her defenses, she missed the plane the first time it flew over. The second time the sound of its engine drew her attention to the vivid blue sky. There was nothing especially unusual about a small plane overhead. Many of the more successful ranchers actually had their own planes to check out the far reaches of their land. Jordan's family was one of them. Many more ranchers hired them on occasion. There was a small but active private airport nearby.

What was unusual about this particular plane was the message trailing through the clear blue sky behind it: Marry Me, Kelly.

She stared at it with a sort of horrified fascination. She supposed a case could be made that it was exactly the sort of impulsive, outrageous thing the old Jordan would have dreamed up, the sort of thing she'd claimed only moments ago to miss. Her heart, in fact, turned a somersault in her chest, a slow loop-de-loop that very nearly made her giddy.

Her gaze riveted on that message, she bit back a groan. The whole blasted county was going to know about Jordan's proposal now. Well, maybe not that Jordan was behind it, though that news would come quickly enough. Los Pinos was small enough that nothing ever stayed secret for long, including the identity of the man who'd taken his family's plane up from the local airstrip to make his proposal in such an outrageous way. Her phone was probably ringing off the hook already.

Even as she watched, the plane made another slow loop and circled back. Just when it reached a spot directly overhead, she saw something being scattered through the sky. Like confetti falling, it drifted down until the first touch of pink landed on her cheek. Rose petals, she realized at its silky touch against her skin. The man had filled the sky with rose petals.

She sucked in a deep breath, inhaling the sweet scent of them, then lowered her head and rode deliberately away from the cascade of pink. Tears stung her eyes. He was making it awfully damned hard to say no. So far, though, he hadn't come close to the one thing that would have guaranteed a *yes*.

She reached the house just in time to see him settling his tall, lanky frame into a rocker on the porch. At the sight of her he stilled and waited, his expression oddly hesitant. That was a new side of Jordan altogether, one that stole her breath away. Not once in all the years she'd known him had he ever appeared the least bit vulnerable. He'd always been terribly, terribly sure of himself.

"You have rose petals in your hair," he said quietly.

"Funny thing about that," she said just as quietly, her gaze caught with his. "They were falling from the sky."

His mouth curved into a slow smile. "Amazing."

"Not many men could make that happen."

"Maybe not. I suppose it takes a man intent on making an impression."

Kelly sighed. "Jordan, you've never needed messages in the sky or rose petals to make an impression on me. Don't you know that?"

He seemed to sense that she hadn't been as impressed as he'd hoped. "What does it take?" he asked.

She reached up and patted his cheek. "I think I'll let you think about that awhile longer."

Undaunted, he followed her into the house, heading straight for the kitchen as always. This time, though, he maneuvered past her and reached for the cups himself. He looked as if he needed to stay occupied, so Kelly washed up at the kitchen sink, then settled herself at the table and waited.

He filled the kettle and put it on the stove, then lingered over her selection of herbal teas. "Which one?"

"Orange spice, I think. The situation seems to call for a little *zing.*"

"What situation would that be?" he inquired, leaning against the counter, his gaze on her steady and unrelenting.

She really hadn't wanted to get into this again today. In fact, she had warned him the topic was off-limits. Those blasted rose petals had made that impossible. "This notion you've gotten in your head," she said.

"About marrying you?"

She grinned at his quick-wittedness. "That's definitely the one. It appears to me that this breakup with Rexanne has hurt you more than you're willing to admit. Perhaps it's addled your brain."

His eyebrows rose a fraction. "Oh, really?"

"Yes, really. Did you really love her, Jordan? Was I mistaken in thinking that she just came along at the right time, at the precise moment when you'd decided you needed a wife to complete your transformation into solid citizen?"

He went very still. "Transformation?"

Kelly almost chuckled at his expression. "I seem to recall a boy who ran away from home at seventeen to be a wildcatter on the oil rigs. Then there was the disruption you caused at the high school when you got on the public address system and performed a rock song you had composed. The lyrics, as I recall, had every teacher blushing. The principal had to take the rest of the day off, she was so stunned. And let's see now, there was the summer you rustled a few of your own daddy's cattle, so you could start your own herd."

A once-familiar impish grin tugged at the corners of his mouth. "Not fair," he accused. "I was only seven when I did that."

"It was, however, the beginning of a highly notable career as the family rebel. I'm sure Harlan despaired of your ever turning into someone respectable." She surveyed him closely, from the neatly trimmed brown hair to the tips of his polished boots, and regretted that his hair no longer skimmed his collar and his boots weren't worn and dusty. "I'd say you beat the odds. A wife would complete the package."

"You make it sound so cold and calculating," he objected.

She shrugged. "If the shoe fits..."

"It doesn't. I'm thirty years old. It's just time I settled down."

"When was it you decided you needed a wife?" she asked.

"What do you mean, when?"

"What was the precise date?"

"I don't recall," he said stiffly. "Sometime last fall, I suppose."

"I'll tell you precisely. It wasn't fall at all. It was January 12, your birthday. You turned thirty with a worse midlife crisis than most men have when they're forty-five. You made your decision. Then you looked around and chose Rexanne. When that didn't work out, you did another survey of the candidates and decided on good old Kelly. Did you figure all alone out here, I wouldn't put up much of a fuss before saying yes?"

He had the grace to look embarrassed by her assessment.

"Well, isn't that exactly how it happened?" she persisted.

"Something like that," he agreed with obvious reluctance. He regarded her with a stubborn thrust of his chin. "That doesn't make the plan any less sound."

"Exactly how far have you thought this through?" she inquired carefully, barely keeping a flare-up of temper in check. "Have you chosen a wedding date? Picked the caterer? Reserved the church?"

"Not exactly," he muttered in a defensive tone, which told her that was exactly what he had done.

She was going to lose it and fling her steaming hot tea straight at him in another ten seconds. "Let me guess," she said. "You were figuring on the same date you'd set with Rexanne and you figured the caterer could just change one of the names on the cake. The minister wasn't likely to care who was standing next to you, isn't that right?"

"Those are just details," he argued. "You can pick the date, the church, the caterer and anything else you want. The sky's the limit."

"How thoughtful!"

"You don't have to be sarcastic."

"Oh, I think I do. When a man gets the romantic notion of letting me fill in for his originally intended bride, I definitely have to get a little sarcastic," she said, clinging to her cup so tightly her knuckles were turning white. The idea of splattering that tea all over him was looking better and better. Unfortunately the stuff was cooling too fast to do much damage and far faster than her temper.

"You have it all wrong," he insisted. "It's not like I plucked your name off some computer network. You and I have known each other all our lives. We're compatible."

"Oh, really?" she said doubtfully. She seized on the most obvious thing she could think of to point out their differences. "Where did you plan on us living?"

He seemed taken aback by the simple question. "In Houston, of course."

"I hate Houston," she shot back.

"No, you don't," he said, as if he knew her better than she did herself. "You just had a bad experience there. Paul colored the way you feel about the city."

Kelly gritted her teeth to control her exasperation. "No," she said eventually, when she could speak calmly. "I disliked it from the first."

"Then why the hell did you move there?"

She would not tell him in a thousand years that she had moved there to be near him. "Because it seemed like the right thing to do at the time. There were opportunities there that didn't exist around here."

"And there still are. Even more doors will open up to you as my wife."

It was the last straw. "Dammit, Jordan, don't you know me at all? I will not use you or anyone else to gain acceptance," she said tightly. "Around here I have made my own way. I have earned the respect people have for me."

"I never said you hadn't," he said. Now his exasperation was clearly growing by the second. "I'm just saying things will be easier for you as my wife."

She sighed. "You'll never get it."

His expression suddenly softened and he hunkered down in front of her. His eyes were level with hers and filled with so much tenderness that Kelly wanted to gaze into them forever. "I do get it," he said quietly. "One of the things I admire most about you is your fierce independence."

"Then how could you even think about taking that away from me and making me nothing more than your appendage?"

His lips quirked with amusement. "Plenty of wives are able to exert their independence. Marriage isn't likely to join two people like us at the hip. I am capable of compromise, Kelly." His gaze caught hers. "Are you?"

The question caught her off guard. "Not if it means losing who I am."

"I want to marry you because of who you are," he declared. "Why would I want you to change?"

"That's what marriage does. It changes people."

"Not if they fight it."

She had no ready answer for that. She was beginning to weaken and he knew it. She could read the gleam of triumph in his eyes. With his hands resting on her thighs, with his masculine scent luring her, all of the old yearnings were beginning. Heat flooded her body and made her reason vanish. She had wanted Jordan Adams as far back as she could remember. She had ached for his touch, hungered for just one of

the wicked kisses that he seemed to share so freely
with other women.

"You've never even kissed me," she murmured
without thinking.

She hadn't meant it as a dare, only as an observation, but Jordan was quick to seize the opening. His
hands, softer now than they had been when he was
working his father's ranch, but still strong, cupped
her face. His thumbs gently grazed her lips until they
parted on a sigh of pure pleasure. His mouth curved
into a half smile at that and, still smiling, he touched
his lips to hers.

The kiss was like the caress of warm velvet, soft and
soothing and alluring. It made her head spin. The
touch of his tongue sent heat spiraling through her,
wicked curls of heat that reached places she was certain had never before been touched.

"Oh, Jordan," she murmured on another sigh as
he gathered her close and deepened the kiss until she
was swimming in a whirlpool of sensation.

In her wildest imagination she hadn't known,
hadn't even guessed at the joy a mere kiss could bring.
This was Jordan, though, the man she'd always believed to be her other half. If she had known his touch
would really be like this, she would have fought for
him long ago. She wouldn't have waited, patient and
silent, for him to wake up and notice her. She would
have overcome her shyness, shoved aside all of her
fears of rejection and tried to seduce him.

If only she were more than a means to an end, if
only he really, truly loved her, she would say yes to

him in a heartbeat, if only to guarantee that incredibly rare moments like this would never end.

When at last he released her, Jordan looked almost as dazed as she felt. His hands lingered on her face as if he couldn't bear to break the contact.

"Was that a *yes?*" he asked.

Kelly listened to her heart and heard *yes* repeated over and over. Her head, though, was louder. "No," she said with more regret than she'd ever felt about anything she'd ever done.

"But..."

She touched a finger to his lips. "Don't argue. This isn't about all the clearheaded, rational arguments you can mount. It's not about bullying me until you get your way."

Jordan looked as lost as if she'd been talking about astrophysics. "What, then?"

"Think about it," she advised him, hiding a grin at his confusion. "I'm sure it will come to you eventually."

Now that he'd really, truly kissed her, now that she knew the first faint stirrings of all the passionate possibilities in his arms, she wasn't sure she'd be able to bear it if it didn't.

Chapter Three

"He is clueless," Kelly declared to Jordan's sister-in-law Jessie a few weeks later.

Kelly hadn't been around when Jessie's marriage to Erik Adams ended with his tragic death in a ranch accident. Jessie had been pregnant with Erik's baby at the time. By the time Kelly had returned to Los Pinos, Luke, the oldest of the Adams brothers, had delivered the baby during a blizzard and he and Jessie had fallen in love and married. Whenever the two of them came home to White Pines with their daughter, Jessie slipped away for a visit and the kind of girl talk they rarely got elsewhere. Over the past months, Kelly had come to consider her a good friend.

"For a man widely regarded as brilliant, I think his synapses regarding women short-circuited sometime around puberty,'' Kelly added as she kneaded her bread dough with a ferocity that had Jessie grinning.

"You love him, though, don't you?" Jessie teased. Regarding Kelly intently, she reached over to still her flour-covered hands.

Kelly gazed into blue eyes filled with concern and sighed heavily. Eventually she drew in a calming breath and shrugged. "Depends on when you ask."

"I'm asking now."

"Now I'm exasperated, annoyed, perplexed and bordering on murderous." Her temper flared up all over again. "He actually thinks I'll pack up Dani and move back to Houston. Wasn't he even awake during my marriage to Paul? Did he miss every single one of the opinions I expressed about the city during the entire drive from Houston back to this ranch? Has he been oblivious to how hard I've worked to make a go of this place? Can't he see how I love it?"

"Maybe he can see that the work is wearing you out. Maybe he just assumes a wife should want to live where her husband lives," Jessie suggested. "There is a tradition of that sort of thing. Whither thou goest, et cetera."

"Well, times have changed. I've been there, done that. I'm perfectly happy right here."

"You look exhausted to me."

"So what? I didn't say it was easy. I said I loved it. Every little improvement I'm able to accomplish around here gives me a deep sense of satisfaction. How can I give that up to go be some socialite wife?"

"It doesn't have to be an either-or situation. Compromise," Jessie said.

"He used the same word, but he doesn't know the meaning of it," Kelly said with conviction. Jordan was the kind of man who knew exactly what he wanted and assumed the rightness of it. Control was second nature to him. He was more like his father in that respect than he had ever acknowledged.

She sighed. "When I came back here after the divorce, I really needed to figure out who I was. I was no longer the teenager with the crush on the boy next door. I was no longer Paul Flint's cheated-on spouse. I didn't know who I was. I'm still rediscovering myself. I don't want to need anyone ever again."

"Then don't marry him."

"Have you ever tried to say no to Jordan?" Kelly inquired dryly. "Short of barring the front door, disconnecting the phone and never looking out the windows, I can't seem to avoid these declarations of intent he's been dreaming up for the past month. Did you look in the living room? There must be seven dozen roses in there. I sneeze when I walk through the door. Worse, Dani's beginning to ask a lot of questions. I've avoided answering them so far, but that can't go on much longer. She's a very perceptive child and all those roses are hard to kiss off." She hesitated. "That's another thing that worries me."

"What?"

"Dani. Jordan acts as if he's scared to death of her sometimes."

Jessie nodded. "I can believe that. The first time he held Angela, he looked as if he might faint. Obviously he's just not used to being around kids."

"Maybe," Kelly said doubtfully. "What if it's more than that? What if he just plain doesn't like children?"

"You asked him to be Dani's godfather. Obviously, you trust him instinctively with your child. Give him time around Dani and see how it goes. How does she behave around him?"

"Dani misses her father desperately. She looks at Jordan with so much hope in her eyes sometimes that it breaks my heart. She wants a daddy. I'm not sure she's too particular about who it is. That's another reason to keep all this nonsense from her. If she learns that Jordan has proposed, she'll stop at nothing to make it happen. Have you ever tried to say no to a stubborn five-year-old? Between worrying about her finding out and fending off Jordan, the whole thing is wearing me out."

"I think it's supposed to wear you down."

Kelly sighed. "That, too."

Jordan was beginning to wonder if Kelly was right, that he had lost his mind. For the past month he'd spent an awful lot of time trying to outguess a woman he had known forever, a woman he'd been certain he understood completely. It was a damned confounding turn of events.

Not that he didn't love a challenge. He did. He'd just never expected his old pal Kelly to provide it. To his everlasting chagrin, he had expected her to say yes to his proposal without giving the matter a second thought. The plan was so sensible, he didn't see how she could say anything else.

As for that kiss they'd shared, his body hardened every time he thought about it. Who would have guessed that good old Kelly had that much passion inside her? Once he'd recovered from the shock, he'd realized that it was a benefit he hadn't even considered when he'd made his choice. Discovering that he wanted her physically was a hell of a bonus.

Years ago, when he'd experienced the first faint stirrings of desire for her, he'd forced them aside. His father had always told him there were women for marrying and women for dalliances. He had known with certainty even then that Kelly was the kind of woman a man married, not the kind he experimented with. That kiss a few weeks back, though, had hinted that she might have shared that early attraction. There had seemed to be a lot of pent-up emotion behind it.

He glanced up just in time to see Ginger taking her usual place on the corner of his desk. Her skirt hitched up a practically indecent three inches, exposing shapely thighs. Her attempt to tug it lower failed dismally. One of these days he really was going to have to have a talk with her about office decorum.

"Don't you ever sit in a chair?" he grumbled.

"Sure," she said easily. "At my desk. At yours, this is better. So, what's it going to be today? Roses? Candy? Balloons? A trip to the moon?"

Jordan sighed. He was running out of ideas. "What would have worked on you?"

"I'm easy. I'd have caved in after the first two or three dozen roses," she said readily. "Of course, DeVonne did have to get a little creative. He actually told me he loved me. Have you mentioned anything along those lines to Kelly?''

He could feel patches of color climbing into his cheeks. Ginger's expression told him she could interpret exactly what that meant. She regarded him with a mix of disgust and pity.

"You haven't, have you? Jordan Adams, you don't deserve a woman like Kelly. You're some kind of throwback to another era. You think you're doing her some great favor just by asking, don't you?''

"Of course not."

Ginger rolled her eyes. "Work on that delivery, boss. It's not believable. You probably told her something romantic like how she'd never have to work another day in her life or how she could attend teas with all the hoity-toity people in Houston society, am I right?''

It was close enough that Jordan could feel another rush of blood up the back of his neck. He scowled at his secretary. "Don't you have work to do?''

"Just taking care of your love life. Once you make up your mind what you're sending today, I'll place the order. Then I'm out of here. I'm taking the afternoon off." Her eyes sparkled with anticipation. "DeVonne is taking me in-line skating tonight. It's our anniversary. I intend to look sexy as hell for the occasion."

"In-line skating? And you call me unromantic," Jordan muttered.

"We met in-line skating," Ginger informed him huffily. "Bumped smack into each other. Believe me, when you smack into a professional linebacker, you're down for the count. When I finally caught my breath, I took one look into those big blue eyes of his and it whooshed straight out of me again. The man is awesome.''

She wagged her pencil at him, obviously hinting she was ready to take notes. "So, what's it going to be today?" she asked again. "Try to be original, boss. Even I'm getting bored and I'm not on the receiving end."

"More roses, I suppose," he said, sounding thoroughly defeated even to his own ears.

Ginger shook her head. "Enough with the roses already. She's bound to be sick of them. I think I'll make it orchids. And if you don't have anything better to do this afternoon, I'd suggest you go to the mall and pick out some outrageously expensive perfume to send tomorrow."

He stared at her blankly. "What kind?"

"Something French and sexy. Something that will drive you wild when you get a whiff of it."

He thought Kelly smelled pretty good as it was, fresh and clean. He wasn't sure he wanted her to smell like a Paris whorehouse. This might be another of those times when it would be best to go with his own instincts and ignore Ginger's. "I'll look around," he promised.

An hour later, after wandering through a mall indecisively, he walked past a lingerie shop. He stopped in his tracks and stared openmouthed at the display in the window. All that silk and lace would definitely drive a man wild. He tried to imagine Kelly's reaction if she opened a box and found something like that inside. Would she slap him upside the head? Laugh at him? Or would her imagination kick into overdrive the way his was doing? Would she finally realize that he truly thought of her as a sexy, provocative woman? He figured it was worth the risk.

After glancing around to see if he was being observed, he sucked in a deep breath and marched inside. He'd never seen so many silky underthings in his life. Each struck him as more daring and sensual than the next.

"May I help you?" a girl barely out of her teens inquired perkily. A Ginger-in-training, he decided.

"I'd like to buy something for a lady."

She grinned. "I'm relieved," she said. "I doubt we'd have anything in your size."

The unexpected joke, which also reminded him of his secretary, released some of his anxiety. "I don't have a clue about sizes and stuff like that," he admitted.

"Is she about my size? Bigger? Smaller?"

"A little taller," he said without hesitation, then paused. The rest seemed downright intimate to be discussing with this total stranger. She was watching him expectantly, though. She was probably used to men fumbling around with embarrassment.

"Maybe a little bigger..." He cleared his throat. "On top," he added in a choked voice.

She grinned again without batting an eye. "Got it. And on the bottom?"

He thought of Kelly's cute, sassy little behind. "Curvy," he said. "But not too big."

The teenager grinned. "Okay. Now, did you want a teddy? A negligee? Bra? Panties?"

He was stymied. His gaze went back to the item that had drawn his attention to the window. Rexanne had owned something similar, but seeing her in it had never seemed to stir him the way just the thought of seeing Kelly wearing one did. He had no idea what it was called.

"What's that?" he asked.

"A teddy. It's from France. Very chic."

Ginger had said he ought to get something from France that was capable of driving him wild. Another glance at the teddy told him that ought to do it. No question about it. With Kelly in it—or mostly out of it—he wouldn't be able to catch his breath for a month.

"I'll take that."

"In red, black, pink or blue?"

"All of them."

The clerk's eyes lit up, which hinted that he might have made a mistake not asking about the price. He didn't care. "Can you wrap them?"

"Absolutely."

Fifteen minutes later he exited the store with his elegantly wrapped package. An hour later he was driving straight toward west Texas at a speed that openly defied state law. This was one gift he intended to give her in person. Tonight. And he was too damned impatient to waste time waiting around in an airport to be on his way. Besides, a long drive was the only way he could think of to cool off before he scared her to death by making it plain exactly how badly he wanted her.

The pounding on the front door woke Kelly from a sound sleep. She glanced at the clock beside her bed. It was well after two in the morning. She automatically sniffed the air for the smell of smoke. A fire was the only thing she could think of that would cause all this uproar at this hour. The air smelled summer fresh with just a hint of the flowers she'd planted in pots on the porch below.

Grabbing her old chenille robe from the foot of the bed, she belted it tightly around her and glanced outside. She spotted Jordan's car parked haphazardly in front of the house. So much for the who, she thought wearily. All that remained was the why. Why would he be carrying on like a lunatic in the middle of the night? She'd sent him a polite thank-you note for the gifts. Maybe he hadn't considered it adequate, but this was hardly an appropriate hour to discuss her lack of manners.

She hurried down the stairs, pausing only to reassure a sleepy-eyed Dani that there was no problem.

"Go on back to bed, sweetie. It's just Jordan."

"He sounds mad or something."

"Don't worry about it. I'll take care of it." In fact, she was going to wring his stupid neck.

Downstairs, she switched on the porch light and opened the door a crack, determined not to admit him. "What do you want?" she demanded, noting that he was still wearing a suit and tie. He had at least loosened the tie. Obviously he'd driven all the way across the state straight from work.

He shoved a huge box toward her. It wouldn't fit through the crack. "I brought you this."

The box was intriguing with its gold paper and fancy bow. Still, Kelly determinedly wrapped her arms around her middle and refused to take it. "Jordan, this has to stop."

Her insistent tone seemed to totally bemuse him. He regarded her with evident confusion. "Why?"

"Because I cannot be bought."

Shock registered on his handsome features. "I'm not trying to buy you," he swore. "I'm trying to..."

Words clearly failed him. Kelly could understand why. There was hardly another interpretation for what he'd been doing. "Buy me," she supplied.

"No," he insisted. "I'm trying to court you."

Her heart skittered wildly. "Oh, Jordan," she murmured, feeling her insides turn to mush. "Please don't do this to me."

His gaze settled on her and a once-familiar warmth spread through her.

"Could I come in so we can discuss this?" he asked.

Kelly did not want him in the house, not with her resolve wavering and his determination solidifying. "It's the middle of the night. I have fences to mend in the morning."

"I'll help," he promised.

"When was the last time you mended a fence?"

"Not that long ago," he shot back. "I was raised on a ranch, you know. There's almost nothing I haven't done."

"And hated," she reminded him. "That's why you couldn't leave White Pines fast enough."

"If you're going to analyze me, could we do it over coffee? I'm beat."

"If you're that tired, go home to White Pines."

"Is there some reason you don't want me in the house?" he inquired, studying her with amusement. "You aren't afraid I'm going to persuade you to say yes, are you?"

That was exactly what she was afraid of, but she refused to admit it. She opened the door wider. "Come on in. You get one cup of coffee and a half hour of my time," she said firmly. "That's it."

He grinned. "Whatever you say."

He was already stripping off his tie on his way to the kitchen. He unbuttoned his collar, exposing a hint of the dark hair on his chest. He sat down, elbows on the table, and watched as she started the coffee. Kelly could feel his gaze on her. When she was sure she was totally composed, thoroughly immune to his charm, she turned toward him.

The speculative, heated look in his eyes made her breath catch in her throat. Nothing, she decided, could have prepared her for that. He looked as if he wanted her, as if he truly desired her, not just as if she were an acquisition he was considering to complete his life. It was a turn of events she definitely hadn't considered.

"Can I talk you into opening your present?" he asked in a slow, lazy tone that made her pulse race.

"No," she said in a rush, her gaze fixed on that lavish box with its fancy wrapping.

"It won't bite," he assured her.

"Jordan, I do not want your presents."

"Not even if giving them to you makes me happy?"

She shook her head. "I should have guessed. We're talking your needs here, not mine."

"You have no idea what I need," he commented, a challenging glint in his eyes. "Want to know?"

Kelly swallowed hard. "I don't think so."

"I'll tell you anyway."

He pulled the box toward him and slipped the ribbon off. He slid a finger under the wrapping paper and flipped it away. Then with the slow, tantalizing timing of a stripper, he lifted the top of the box. Kelly couldn't have shifted her gaze away if her life had depended on it.

He folded back the layers of tissue paper and hooked a finger through a narrow strap of red silk. As he lifted his hand, the sexiest, most exquisite teddy she had ever seen emerged from the box. She felt his gaze on her, gauging her reaction. She couldn't stop looking at that obviously outrageously expensive scrap of lace and silk. She thought of all the plain cotton underthings in her drawers upstairs. She wanted that teddy with every feminine fiber of her being. She stared at it, trying to hide her longing.

That, she thought, swallowing hard, was what he saw when he looked at her? When had he stopped thinking of her as denim and plaid? When had he stopped looking at her as a pal and begun noticing her as a woman?

"It's...beautiful," she said in a choked voice, reaching out to skim her fingers over the silk. She jerked her hand back as if that red-as-flame material were just as hot as any blaze, except perhaps the one inside her.

"There are more," he said, dropping the teddy he held into a pool of red on the table.

Sinful black followed, then a wild, hot shade of pink. The last was a vivid, sapphire blue. Kelly loved them all. Never in her life had she owned anything quite so provocative. Her wardrobe of underwear tended toward practical cotton, with a few scraps of lace and silk for special occasions, but there was nothing, *nothing* like this. It hadn't seemed necessary since she and Paul had split. Indulgences were something she couldn't afford.

"Where on earth would I wear them?" she murmured, even as she clutched them to her.

"Why not here?" he asked. "The thought of one of these under your jeans and an old plaid shirt gives me goose bumps."

"It's not very practical," she said.

"Not everything in life has to be practical," he reminded her.

"It does when you're trying to keep a ranch afloat."

"Then think of me as the impractical side of your life." He gestured around the kitchen with its faded wallpaper, old appliances and huge oak table. "All of this represents reality. Let me fulfill your dreams."

Tears sprang to her eyes at the sweet, tempting suggestion. "Jordan, sometimes you say the most incredible things," she said.

He seemed alarmed that she was crying. His finger shook as he wiped away the dampness on her cheeks. "Sweetheart, I didn't mean to make you cry."

"I know," she said, crying harder, then laughing at herself. "It's so silly. You're making it so hard for me to go on saying no."

"That's the idea."

"One of us has to be practical here. Obviously it's not going to be you. Jordan, it wouldn't work," she repeated for what seemed the hundredth time. This time, though, even she could tell there was a lot less conviction behind the declaration.

"We're not a couple of kids with stars in our eyes," he said. "We could make it work."

The remark, so like him, snapped her out of the dreamy, hopeful state of mind he'd induced in her. "But I want stars in my eyes. If I ever marry again, I want it all." She fingered the piles of silk scattered across the table, then gazed directly into his eyes. "I want it all, Jordan. Nothing less."

He stood slowly, then, the faintest hint of anger in his eyes. "I won't stop trying," he said with a touch of defiance.

"You'll be wasting your time."

Before she realized what he intended, he turned back, leaned down and kissed her, a bruising, hard kiss that stole her breath away. His mouth plundered hers, branding her as his as surely as if she'd been one of those heads of cattle at White Pines.

While she was still dazed, he said softly, "I don't think so, sweetheart. I don't think it will be a waste of time at all."

Chapter Four

Jordan figured he must have gotten less than an hour of sleep the entire night. Despite his exhaustion, he was back at Kelly's just before dawn, expecting to find her dressed and ready to get to all that fence mending she'd talked about the night before. Instead he found the house quiet and dark except for a faint light he thought he detected in the kitchen.

So, she hadn't gotten much sleep, either. He counted that as a positive sign, an indication that perhaps she had spent the remaining hours of the night lying awake thinking about him, just as he had about her.

He walked around toward the back of the house, prepared to taunt her a little about getting a late start. Instead he found only Dani in the kitchen, standing on a chair in front of the sink, carefully pouring cereal into a bowl.

Hiding his disappointment, he tapped on the screen door. When Dani turned toward him and her face lit up, he felt the oddest sensation in the pit of his stomach. It was almost... *paternal,* he thought with amazement, or at least what he took to be some sort of fatherly emotion. Relief that he could experience such a sensation flooded through him. It would certainly make his future with Kelly less complicated.

"Hi, Jordan. Want some breakfast?"

Stepping inside, he eyed the frosted cereal warily. "I don't think so."

"It's really, really good."

She looked so hopeful that he relented. "Okay, maybe just a little."

She stretched on tiptoe, teetering just enough to cause his breath to catch in his throat. Reaching into the cupboard, she withdrew another bowl, a very large bowl. Then she upended the box and dumped in enough cereal to feed an army.

"Hey," he protested, "I said a little bit."

She gave him another of those disarming smiles. "I think you're going to really, really like it."

Leaving the box on the counter, she climbed down while Jordan held his breath and barely restrained the urge to pluck her up and set her feet firmly on the floor himself. He did manage to grab the bowls before she could and put those safely on the table.

She retrieved a carton of milk from the refrigerator and a pair of spoons from a drawer. It seemed to be a routine with which she was disturbingly familiar. It gave him yet another argument to use on Kelly. If they were married, she wouldn't be out of the house so much or so exhausted that her daughter was up before her, as he suspected might be the case this morning. At any rate, if he had his way, Dani would have a full-time mother.

"All set?" he inquired dryly, watching her precise preparations.

Looking an awful lot like her mother had years ago, she bit her lower lip and studied the table thoughtfully. "We need a banana," she decided.

She scampered into the pantry and returned with a banana. With surprisingly deft little fingers, she peeled it, broke it almost in two and plopped the larger piece into his bowl and kept the smaller for herself.

"Maybe we should slice it," Jordan observed.

"I can't. Mommy doesn't let me use knives when she's not here."

"Then it's a good thing I'm here," he said. He opened a drawer and retrieved one.

"How come you know where the knives are?"

"Because I'll bet I've been in this kitchen almost as many times as you have," he told her.

She tilted her head and studied him suspiciously. "How come? I live here."

He grinned at her. "Ah, yes, but I grew up practically next door and I was over here almost every day when your mom and I were kids. Nothing much has changed in here."

"Oh, yeah, I forgot. You've known Mommy a really, really long time."

"Forever," he agreed, surprised at how easily conversation came with this pint-size version of his oldest friend. Why had he never noticed before that Dani wasn't really so terrifying? She was just a little person with obvious views already forming. He already knew about her powers of persuasion.

"Speaking of your mom, where is she this morning? Still sleeping?"

"No. She left a long time ago. She's mending fences right outside. She says I can come find her when I'm done with breakfast." She eyed him speculatively. "Maybe you should come, too. Can you string wire?"

"With the best of them," he affirmed.

She gave a little satisfied nod. "Good, because I can't really help. Mommy's afraid I'll get barbed wire stuck in my backside."

"A very real danger," Jordan said, trying not to chuckle out loud. He took his first tentative bite of cereal. To a man whose cereal consumption was usually confined to bran flakes, this stuff was sweet enough to make him gag. He noticed that Dani was watching him intently, a worried frown puckering her brow.

"Don't you like it?" she asked, sounding like an uncertain cook whose very first meal was on the table.

"It's…" He struggled to find a word that wouldn't offend, but also wouldn't encourage her to offer him more—ever. "It's different."

She gave a tiny sigh of resignation. "Too sweet, huh?"

"A little bit," he confirmed.

"That's what Mommy says, too. She says it makes her gag. I only get to have it on weekends, so it won't destroy my brain cells."

Jordan grinned. "I don't think your brain cells are in any immediate danger. You seem pretty bright to me."

"Thank you," she said politely.

They ate their cereal in companionable silence after that. The instant Dani had finished hers, she picked up the bowl and carried it back to the sink and climbed deftly back onto the same chair so she could reach the faucets. She rinsed the bowl and stacked it in the drainer. Jordan carried his own bowl to the sink.

"I'll wash it for you," the child offered.

"No way," he said. "Fair's fair. You fixed breakfast. I can at least wash my own bowl."

Dani climbed down without argument. "I'll go brush my teeth and then we can go." She eyed him worriedly again. "Do you have a toothbrush with you? Mommy says it's important to brush your teeth at least twice a day, especially after breakfast, so your teeth won't rot."

"After all that sugar, I can see why it would be a concern," Jordan agreed. "Don't worry about me, though, I'll take care of my teeth."

"You won't leave without me, will you?"

"Nope. I'll be waiting right here."

"Maybe you'd like to see the kittens before we go," she said hopefully. "They're getting really, really big. You might want one, after all. Mr. Adams is taking the tiger-striped one, so you can't have him. And Jessie said she'd take the black-and-white one."

Jordan hid a grin. Obviously his whole family had been taken in by this little con artist. "Did you manage to pawn one off on Cody?"

"Oh, yeah. I forgot. He said he'd take the two that look like twins. They're black with little white noses."

"Two, huh? You must have been very persuasive."

"Not me," she said modestly. "It was the kittens. I told you they're really, really cute. I think you're going to change your mind."

"I don't think so, but we can take a look after we help your mom."

"Okay," she agreed, and ran off, her tiny feet thundering up the stairs.

Jordan shook his head. Maybe kids weren't so mysterious, after all. Maybe, like grown-ups, they just wanted someone to listen and take them seriously. More or less the way he wanted Kelly to take him seriously. Though she hadn't exactly laughed in his face, she didn't seem to think anything he had to say on the subject of marriage was worth listening to. He had to come up with some way to change that before this unexpected desire he'd begun feeling for her drove him out of his mind.

Before he could come up with a new twist on what already seemed like an old theme, Dani raced back down the stairs.

"Let's go."

"Do you know exactly where your mom's working?" he asked, wondering a bit at Kelly's willingness to leave Dani all alone.

"Sure. She's right behind the barn."

About a hundred yards away, more or less, easily within shouting distance. Which meant, Jordan thought dryly, she had definitely seen or at least heard him arrive. Which also meant she was deliberately avoiding him, he concluded with an odd sense of triumph. Kelly only hid out when she was uncertain. Her resolve must be wavering.

With Dani leading the way, they circled around the barn. He spotted Kelly less than a hundred yards along the fence line, the sunlight glistening off her hair. Despite the heat, she was wearing a long-sleeved blouse, jeans and heavy gloves to protect herself from the barbed wire. Even so, as they approached, he could see a rip in one sleeve and a tiny nick on her flushed cheek.

An irrational surge of anger boiled up inside him, followed rapidly by a tide of protectiveness. She shouldn't be doing this. Even if she insisted on ranching, she should have a foreman and half a dozen hands to deal with the heavy labor. He knew in his gut, though, that she wouldn't thank him for suggesting that. With that damned pride of hers, she wanted to do it all herself. It was as much a matter of principle with her as it was a financial necessity.

"Hi, Mommy," Dani shouted, running ahead. "Jordan's here to help."

Kelly's head snapped up at the sound of her daughter's voice, then her gaze sought his. He could see the dark circles under her eyes and knew at once that he was responsible. Oddly, though, he didn't feel the same sense of triumph he'd felt earlier when he'd suspected she might have spent the same sort of restless night he had. This was the reality. She looked exhausted. And on a ranch, people who were exhausted could make dangerous mistakes, as he knew only too well. A careless mistake was what had cost them his brother Erik, when his tractor had overturned at Luke's.

"Damn," he muttered under his breath. He should never have let this happen.

He approached her slowly, then hunkered down next to her. He touched a finger to the torn sleeve, but his gaze went at once to her cheek. The nick there was as tiny as he'd first suspected, but it had bled. "You should clean that out."

"It's nothing," she said, avoiding his gaze. "I'm up-to-date on my tetanus shots. I'll wash it out and put some peroxide on it when I go inside. What are you doing here?"

"I told you I'd be back to help with the fences."

"It's not necessary."

"A promise is a promise." He stood and slid his hands into the pockets of an old pair of jeans he hadn't worn in years and rocked back on his heels.

She fell silent and, for the life of him, Jordan couldn't think of another thing to say, either. He wondered why after years of having so much to talk about, they were suddenly so awkward with each other. The quiet serenity he'd come to count on had vanished. If it was lost forever, he had no one to blame but himself. He'd tried to change things between them and in doing so had cost himself the one thing that had mattered most—Kelly's friendship.

With Dani assigned to walk along the fence line to look for additional breaks, Jordan was left alone with Kelly.

"Get much sleep last night?" he asked eventually.

"Enough," she replied tightly, concentrating on her struggle to stretch the next length of wire taut.

Jordan leaned down to help her. "Doesn't look that way to me," he observed.

She scowled at him. "Thank you."

He grinned at the testy note. "Not that you're not always beautiful," he told her.

She glanced up, her face just inches under his. The nearness was too tempting for Jordan to resist. He dropped a quick kiss on the tip of her nose.

"Jordan!" she warned, casting a harried look in Dani's direction.

"She might as well get used to it," he said. "The same goes for you."

"Not now," she snapped impatiently, jerking on the wire. She lost her grip and the line snapped back, snagging her sleeve. She muttered a colorful expletive under her breath as Jordan reached for her hand.

"Let me see."

"No. It's nothing."

He chuckled, suddenly recalling how often she had reacted just that way to any hint of sympathy whenever she'd taken a spill from a horse or scraped her knees when they were up to their childhood pranks.

"You never did want anyone fussing over you," he said, capturing her hand despite her attempts to avoid his grasp. He couldn't feel the warmth of her skin or its silky smoothness through the thick gloves, but he could imagine it. His body tightened.

"I still don't," she said heatedly.

Jordan ignored the protest and her squirming as he examined the rip in her sleeve and checked to see if the wire had snagged the tender skin beneath. "Just a scratch," he said eventually.

"I told you that."

"Yes, but your diagnosis wasn't nearly as informed as mine. I actually checked your arm."

"Jordan, I was working this fence line long before you showed up this morning and I will be working it long after you're back in your penthouse office in Houston next week."

"Can't deny that," he said agreeably. "But while I'm here, you might as well let me pitch in."

She rocked back on her haunches and sighed. The look she turned on him was filled with exasperation and resignation. "On one condition."

He grinned. "I love it when you bargain."

She fought a smile and eventually succumbed. "Do you have any idea what a perverse man you are?"

"Is that good?"

"I've certainly never considered it to be a desirable attribute."

"Then I'll change," he promised.

"Pardon me if I don't hold my breath. As for that condition, you will not under any circumstances bring up that ridiculous proposal while Dani's in the vicinity. Got it?'' she asked, regarding him with a defiant lift of her chin.

''Why not?''

''Isn't that obvious? I don't want her getting ideas about the two of us. She'll only be disappointed.''

Jordan glanced up and searched for some sign of Dani. The fence line apparently forgotten, she was gathering wildflowers. She had an armload. He was struck by a sense of déjà vu.

''Looks as if she has your taste in floral displays,'' he commented, directing Kelly's attention to her daughter. As he did, he realized where he'd gone wrong. He'd been trying to woo Kelly the same way he would court those shallow, grasping socialites in Houston. Kelly wasn't a hothouse-flower kind of woman. Bluebells or daisies would have pleased her more.

Now that the realization had come to him, he saw that it had always been true. Her favorite gifts as a teenager hadn't been the fancy ones he and his brothers and their friends brought to her birthday parties. She'd always loved most the ones her father and mother had made for her, gifts that had come from the heart.

What could he give her now that would have the same kind of meaning? He studied her as she watched her daughter, saw the delight and love shining in her eyes, and recalled how often she'd worried out loud to him about the absence of Paul Flint in Dani's life. ''She needs her father,'' she had said more than once.

Jordan wasn't convinced that anyone on earth needed a man like Paul Flint, but Kelly's point had registered just the same. She wanted her daughter to have a daddy. Even his father had seen that.

If Jordan could prove to her that he was suited for that role, if he could give her what she wanted most for her child, maybe Kelly would finally accept the idea that she needed him as a husband, as well.

Kelly watched as the sun beat down on Jordan's bare shoulders. He'd stripped off his shirt an hour or so before and she hadn't gotten a thing done since. Every once in a while she managed to tear her gaze away after giving herself a stern lecture about turning into a sex-starved divorcée, but in general she found the play of his gleaming muscles entrancing.

How on earth did he stay so fit sitting in an office all day long? she wondered. His shoulders and chest were thicker than she'd recalled, no longer an adolescent boy's body, but a man's. An intriguing line of dark hair arrowed down his washboard-flat stomach and vanished beneath the snap of his faded, snug jeans.

For years now she had forbidden herself to study him with so much carnal fascination. First of all, she had been married and she would have died before allowing herself even a hint of disloyalty toward a man she'd belatedly discovered didn't deserve it.

Then, more recently, it had seemed like a very bad idea to allow her old feelings for Jordan to stir to life again. She hadn't needed the pain of another rejection. He'd never given her a second glance during all those years when she had worn her heart on her sleeve. There was no reason to believe his feelings toward her had changed.

Now, though, with his proposal on the table—albeit for all the wrong reasons—she felt she had a right to study him from his windblown hair to his dusty boots. The sight of that expensive snakeskin layered with barnyard dirt made her smile. This was the old Jordan, the one she'd missed, the one who didn't give a hang about appearances. The most rebellious of the brothers who'd filled the days of the lonely, only child next door, allowing her to tag along with them and later to compete with them as an equal.

"What are you looking at so intently?" he inquired, his voice laced with amusement.

She could feel herself blushing to the roots of her hair. "I was just worried you were going to mar that beautiful expanse of chest."

His gaze settled on her. "Would you have kissed it to make it better? It might have been worth it."

Dazed by the very idea, she slowly shook her head. "I don't think so," she said in a choked voice.

"Why not?"

"Bad idea," she mumbled, forcing herself to look away.

"What was that?" he taunted.

She stared at him defiantly. "I said you're a flirt and a tease and proper women aren't safe around you."

He nodded seriously. "I thought it might be something like that."

"Don't sound so proud of yourself."

He winked at her. "I'm not the only one around here for whom pride is a character defect."

"Jordan, I..." Her voice trailed off. There was no point in arguing with him, no point in trying to explain that pride wasn't keeping her from accepting his proposal. It just wouldn't work. She couldn't marry a man she loved so desperately and spend the rest of her life pretending that she didn't.

Still, knowing that the one thing she'd always dreamed about—marrying Jordan—was finally within her reach and yet so far away, filled her with wistfulness.

She was so lost in imagining a life with Jordan that she never noticed that the sun was beginning to sink toward the horizon in a blaze of orange. When she felt a shadow fall over her, she looked up and saw Jordan staring down at her. He'd shrugged into his shirt, but left it unbuttoned. The impish gleam that had been in his eyes all day had given way to a look that was far hotter and more dangerous.

When he held out his hand to assist her up, Kelly briefly considered ignoring it. Something inside her, though, longed for some contact, no matter how innocent. His earlier inspection of her arm had made her heart pound. Her blood had sizzled with the memory of his quick, unexpected kiss on the tip of her nose and, despite her best intentions, she wanted him to repeat it.

No, she corrected, what she wanted was a repeat of that spine-tingling kiss they'd shared in her kitchen a month ago. There had been the kind of magic in that kiss she could almost believe in. It was the kind of magic that could make a woman forget that she'd ever been betrayed by a man. It was the kind that inspired wonder and hope for the future. It was the dangerous kind.

Sighing, she put her hand in his and let him help her up. Her muscles ached. Her eyes were scratchy from dust and exhaustion. Her nose felt sunburned, despite repeated applications of lotion and the hat that she'd tried to keep on but had tossed aside more than once as a nuisance.

"Tired?" Jordan asked, his gaze warm and filled with concern.

"A bit," she admitted, wondering at the expression in his eyes that said he thought she was beautiful, despite what she knew to be the truth after a long day of hard work under a hot sun.

"Then I'll take charge of the rest of the night. Shower and change, then you and I and Dani will go into town for pizza."

She stared at him in openmouthed astonishment. She doubted Jordan had dined on pizza since he'd discovered French cuisine and four-star restaurants. And he had never, ever, indicated the slightest desire to spend any more time than absolutely necessary with her daughter.

"You want to take both of us into town for pizza," she repeated, not bothering to hide her incredulity.

"You haven't changed that much, have you? You still love pizza?"

"Of course, but..."

"And Dani?"

"It's her favorite."

"Well, then, it's all settled. I'll be back to get you in an hour." He dropped another one of those innocuous pecks on her nose and headed for his car, leaving her staring after him in bemusement.

Exactly when, she wondered, had her old buddy—steady, safe, reliable Jordan—become so unpredictable? One thing was for certain, the evidence that he had was definitely mounting up.

Chapter Five

The aroma of garlic and oregano, of tomato sauce and spicy Italian sausage filled the tiny pizza parlor in town. Kelly had taken Dani to DiPasquali's Italian Kitchen only occasionally. The visits had been a rare treat on their tight budget. Even so, the old wooden booths with their red vinyl seats, the scarred tables and red-checked napkins were very familiar. They hadn't changed at all since she and Jordan and their friends had come here as teenagers. Just walking through the door evoked all sorts of fond memories.

The owners were the same, as well. Anthony and Gina DiPasquali were still fussing over their customers as they had for three decades now. Now their daughter Liz and their son Tony were slowly taking over the business, but it was Anthony's boisterous command of a kitchen that turned out consistently mouth-watering pizza and Gina's warmth that drew people back.

Gina had obviously caught a glimpse of Jordan even before they came through the door. She was already rushing out from behind the register as they entered. She threw open her arms to envelop him in a smothering hug that had Kelly grinning and Jordan looking faintly embarrassed.

"How many years has it been since you've come to see me?" Gina demanded after a spate of Italian delivered with a Texas twang. No one knew for certain which language was her first, English or Italian, but she managed to keep up a steady stream in both. "I'll tell you how many. Too many. Come, come. You will sit at our very best table, right beside the kitchen so I can visit with you when it is quiet and Anthony can see you as he goes in and out."

When Kelly, Dani and Jordan were settled in the booth, Gina beamed at them. "It is like old times, yes? The two of you here together. Now, tell me, what can I get you? Is it still the large pizza with everything and the largest soft drinks in the house?"

"No anchovies," Kelly reminded her emphatically.

"And I'd like a beer," Jordan added.

She smiled down at Dani. "And for you, little one? A small soda, perhaps?"

Dani shook her head. "A big one, just like them."

Kelly grinned at her daughter. "I think a small might be better. You can have more if you want it."

Dani sighed heavily. "Okay, Mommy."

Jordan laughed. At a quizzical look from Kelly, he said, "She reminds me so much of you. Sometimes it's spooky. It takes me back so many years."

Suddenly nostalgic, Kelly asked, "They were good times, weren't they, Jordan?"

He reached across the table and captured her hand in his. "The best."

Dani studied them intently, moving from Kelly's face to Jordan's and back again. "Tell me," she insisted. "Tell me about way back then."

Jordan finally released her hand and leaned back in the booth. "It wasn't that long ago, munchkin," he informed Dani indignantly. "Your mom and I are hardly old codgers."

"What's a codger?"

Kelly grinned at Jordan's apparent loss for words. Obviously he wasn't used to a five-year-old's insistence on explanations for everything she didn't understand. *Why* and *how come* were among Dani's favorite words.

"A codger," she explained, "is a cranky old person."

Dani nodded sagely. "Okay, you aren't that cranky, I suppose. Except when I forget and leave my markers all over the floor and you slip and fall down."

"Yes," Kelly admitted. "I am definitely cranky then." She leaned close to her daughter's perfect face. "But I am not old!"

"How old are you?"

"You know," Kelly said, not particularly wanting to be reminded that she would turn thirty in a few months. If she had the same kind of early mid-life crisis Jordan had experienced, who knew what craziness she was likely to indulge in.

Dani looked at Jordan. "You know how old she is. Tell me," she commanded with all the imperiousness at her disposal.

Jordan waggled a finger to encourage her to come closer. Dani knelt on the seat and leaned across the table.

"She is almost thirty," he confided in a stage whisper.

"Isn't that old?" Dani asked.

"Very, very old," he confirmed.

"You'll pay for that," Kelly warned him. She couldn't really get angry at the lighthearted byplay. Watching the exchange between her daughter and Jordan warmed her heart. If only... She brought herself up short. That way lay heartache.

Jordan looked intrigued by her mild threat. "Oh?"

"When you least expect it," she added.

"Something to look forward to," he noted, clearly not the least bit worried.

A slow, lopsided grin crept across his face. There was a knowing twinkle in his eyes that made Kelly's stomach flip over. Obviously she'd chosen to taunt a master and he'd managed to turn the tables on her with no more than a dangerous look.

The moment might have lasted far longer, if Dani hadn't grown impatient at being ignored. She tugged on Jordan's sleeve. "What was the baddest thing Mommy ever did?"

His eyes were still sparkling. This time, though, it was clearly at some memory Kelly had the feeling she didn't want him sharing with her precocious daughter. Thankfully, Anthony came out of the kitchen just then with their pizza. Kelly prayed that the distraction would get Dani's mind off the past.

It worked, too, for another five minutes. Long enough for Dani to take her first bite of pizza and her first sip of soft drink. Long enough for Anthony and Jordan to spend time catching up, before Anthony retreated to the kitchen. Long enough for Kelly's nerves to get entirely rattled in anticipation of which memories were crowding into Jordan's head and which he might choose to share.

Lord knew, she had her own. She remembered lazy summer days beside the creek, fishing poles in hand, as she and Jordan talked about their hopes and dreams. She'd been the first he'd told about his hunger to work the oil fields. She recalled winter skating parties at the same creek, with a bonfire and mugs of hot chocolate and Jordan's arm casually thrown around her shoulders to keep warm. She recalled the two of them racing each other and the wind on horseback. Jordan always won, but it was the ride itself that was exhilarating, that and being with the boy she knew she loved.

Sometimes it seemed what she remembered most was the sense of anticipation, the belief that at any second Jordan would look into her eyes and discover the woman he loved. She remembered, too, the bitter disappointment at each and every lost opportunity. More, she'd never forgotten the sense of having failed dismally because not even the man who knew her best wanted her.

"Tell me, Jordan."

Dani's command cut through her reverie and Kelly studied the two people she loved most in the world. Dani had a streak of tomato sauce on her face and a faint soda mustache. Jordan wore a faded chambray shirt, open at the collar. He hadn't bothered to tame his hair into the style he wore in Houston. Just from the one day in the sun, she thought she could detect blond highlights scattered in the rich brown. A few more days of outside work and it would be streaked with lighter strands.

Her gaze dropped to his hands, already sporting the beginnings of a golden tan. She knew the strength of those hands. For years, it seemed, she had longed to feel them caressing her, had dreamed of them waking her senses. Instead, it had been Paul Flint's rougher touch that had awakened her sexuality.

"Well, now," Jordan began with a touch of drama in his voice as he responded to Dani's insistent demand. He glanced into Kelly's eyes and a smile curved the corners of his mouth. "Did you know that your mother once locked me in the attic?"

"I did not," Kelly retorted indignantly, recalling the incident vividly, but with a decidedly different spin.

"Did, too," he accused.

"The door stuck. That wasn't my fault."

"You were the one who slammed it so hard it rattled the hinges."

"Because you were tormenting me."

Jordan had the same innocent expression on his face now that he'd had then when he'd explained to her parents why he was hidden away in their attic after suppertime. He'd told only part of the story, just enough to worry her, just enough to get her and not himself into trouble. Kelly scowled at him. "You were a brat then and you're a brat now."

Dani's fascinated gaze clung to Jordan. "What happened then? Did Mommy get punished?"

"She did, indeed," Jordan said with an expression of smug satisfaction on his face. "She was grounded for a whole week and she had to clean the attic. She hated that the most because it was all dusty and covered in cobwebs."

"You mean, there were spiders?" Dani asked. At his nod, she said, "Ugh! That's disgusting." She glanced worriedly at Kelly. "You wouldn't make me clean the attic, would you?"

"Depends on whether you're ever bad," Kelly declared, purposely injecting an ominous note into her voice.

"I'm never bad," Dani protested. "Well, hardly ever and I never, ever, locked anyone in the attic."

"Then we won't have a problem, will we? Now then, I think that's enough reminiscing for one night. I think it's time we were getting home."

As they were driving back to the ranch, Kelly sensed Jordan's gaze on her. He'd been in an odd mood ever since they'd left the restaurant, a little withdrawn, maybe a little nostalgic.

"Do you remember what I was tormenting you about that day in the attic?" he inquired eventually in a lazy drawl.

Kelly glanced into the back seat and saw that Dani had fallen asleep. "I remember," she admitted. Even now the memory had her scowling. "You wanted to practice kissing."

"I wanted to be sure I got it right. I didn't want to kiss my first date and get it wrong. It would have been humiliating."

"And kissing me wrong wouldn't have bothered you?" she inquired just as irritably now as she had then.

"Nope. I knew you'd forgive me. I was trusting you with my fragile ego."

"Do you have any idea how infuriating it was to a teenage girl to be considered target practice for some boy? What you were telling me was that I was not good enough for the real thing."

His expression sobered. "I never meant for you to see it that way."

Unexpected tears gathered in her eyes. "Then why would you be doing the same thing to me now?" she asked quietly.

He looked over at her, shock written all over his face. "What the hell is that supposed to mean?"

"Aren't you asking to practice marriage on me, just the way you did with kissing back then?"

"Of course not!"

"Sounds that way to me."

"Marrying you won't be practice, Kelly. It'll be for keeps."

He said it so emphatically that she almost believed him. Still, there was no getting around the point that he had never once, not in all the years she'd known him, said he loved her. Even Paul Flint had given her that much. Maybe the words hadn't meant much in the end, but at least they'd started off with a promise of undying love. If that hadn't been enough to sustain a marriage, how could she possibly trust a commitment that started with anything less?

After he'd dropped Kelly and Dani off, Jordan drove home, pondering the evening. He wasn't exactly sure where he'd gone wrong. He'd thought the entire day was going really well. He'd actually enjoyed being with Dani, answering her endless questions, awestruck by her inquisitiveness. He'd loved teasing bright patches of indignant color into Kelly's too pale cheeks. He'd thought the taunting and the memories had stirred exactly the right kind of amorous thoughts.

But there had been no mistaking the sudden souring of the mood on the drive home. He had no idea how to combat this absurd notion Kelly had gotten that he viewed a marriage between them as practice. That wasn't it at all. When he made a commitment, he kept it. Businessmen he dealt with trusted him on the basis of a handshake. Why couldn't a woman he'd known all his life trust him on the basis of a sacred vow?

He was still mulling over what had happened when he glanced into his rearview mirror and noted a pair of headlights bearing down on his car. Whoever it was was driving erratically and far too fast given the nighttime conditions on the winding country road. Jordan clung to the wheel a little more tightly.

There was a sharp curve coming up just ahead and even though he knew the road like the back of his hand, he felt his palms turn sweaty. That curve was no place to be with a crazy driver on his tail. Opting not to take a chance, he pulled off onto the shoulder of the road to let the car pass. As it whizzed by, he realized with a sense of dismay that the bright red pickup was Cody's.

"What the hell?" he muttered, pulling out behind his brother and speeding up a little.

The truck took the curve on two wheels, causing Jordan's breath to lodge in his throat. A sense of impending tragedy made his stomach tighten. Dear God in heaven, he wasn't sure the family could take another loss. Erik's death had shaken them all, especially Luke, who had been there when that tractor overturned, and their father. Harlan Adams was tough, but they had all known he felt a terrible burden of responsibility for not recognizing that Erik wasn't suited for ranch work. If anything happened to Cody on the heels of that, it would destroy him.

Staying a safe distance behind—not that he was willing to drive fast enough to catch his brother—he followed him all the way to the turnoff that led to the small house Cody had built for himself a few miles from the main house at White Pines.

Dust churned and rocks flew on the unpaved lane. By the time Jordan pulled to a stop, Cody had already leapt from the truck and stormed into the house.

Whatever had him in such a state must have been pretty bad, Jordan surmised. He'd left the truck door and the front door of the house standing wide open. Just to be on the safe side, Jordan leaned inside the truck and nabbed the keys Cody had left in the ignition. His brother wasn't getting back on the road tonight, if he had anything to say about it.

Jordan approached the house cautiously and peered inside. "Cody?"

The sound of objects slamming against walls carried from the bedroom. He followed the clatter. The sight that greeted him almost made his heart stop. Cody's face was twisted in fury. When he wasn't throwing lamps and boots against the wall, he was haphazardly jamming clothes into two open suitcases on the bed. He was cursing a blue streak at the same time.

Jordan tried to make sense of what he was saying, but other than gathering it had something to do with Melissa Horton, the rest was lost in a tangle of expletives.

"Cody!" He had to shout to make himself heard over the racket his brother was making.

Cody whirled as if he'd been shot. "What the hell do you want?" he demanded. "Who let you in?"

"Since there's no one here except you and me, I guess the answer to that is obvious," he said lightly, hoping to calm his younger brother down by staying cool himself. "So, what's going on?"

"What does it look like?"

"It would appear that you're packing."

"A hell of an observation. No wonder they pay you big bucks in Houston."

"Want to tell me what this is all about?"

"Not particularly. I just want to hit the road."

"To go where?"

Cody paused for a minute and a fleeting expression of indecision passed over his face. It was rapidly chased away by an all-too-familiar look of stubborn defiance. It was the one trait the Adams men shared in spades.

"Who knows?" he said.

"Sounds like you've really thought this through," Jordan commented dryly.

"Look, I didn't invite you here," Cody snapped. "And I don't need to listen to any of your pompous sermons."

"You must have me confused with Daddy."

Cody almost grinned at that, then caught himself. "Jordan, just stay out of this, okay?" he said in a calmer, more resigned tone. "Please."

"I don't think I can do that. You're obviously upset about something, too upset to be taking off without thinking things through."

Cody slammed the suitcases shut and headed for the door. "Your opinion is duly noted," he said as he exited.

Jordan watched him go and counted to ten. Cody tore through the front door, steaming mad.

"What have you done with my keys?"

"Tucked them away for safekeeping," he admitted. "I saw the way you were driving earlier. You're not getting back on the road until you cool down."

Cody crossed the room in three strides and stood toe-to-toe with him. Cody was only an inch or so taller, but he was broader through the shoulders. If it had been anyone other than his brother, Jordan might have been intimidated. With Cody, though, he stood his ground. There was too much at stake for him to back down now. He was willing to risk a black eye and a tender jaw, if that's what it took to keep him here, at least for tonight.

"Give me the keys," Cody demanded, his hands balling into fists.

Jordan met his furious gaze evenly. "I can't do that," he said softly. "You know I can't, Cody."

Apparently Cody recognized the note of determination in his voice. As if he were a balloon that had been punctured, Cody seemed to deflate before his eyes. He combed his fingers through his hair and sighed. "Damn."

"Come on, little brother. Sit down and tell me what this is all about," Jordan encouraged. "Did you and Daddy have a fight? You know how muleheaded he is. He'll give in eventually, though."

"This isn't about Daddy." Cody's mouth twisted in a mockery of a smile. "For a change."

"Melissa?"

There was a haunted look in Cody's eyes when he finally lifted his head and met Jordan's gaze. "I caught her out with my best friend," he admitted. Every painful word seemed to be wrenched from deep inside him.

"Maybe it was totally innocent," Jordan said, standing up for the girl he knew absolutely worshiped his brother.

"Trust me, that's not the case," Cody said bitterly. "They were in each other's arms. They didn't have to spell it out for me."

"So you're going to run off and leave the field open for him to move in on her?"

"I'd say it's a bit late to be worrying about him moving in. He's claimed her as his already."

"I don't believe it," Jordan said emphatically. "She's crazy about you."

"Maybe she was," Cody conceded. "Not anymore."

Jordan saw the anguish the admission cost him. Everyone in the family had teased Cody at one time or another about taking Melissa for granted. It appeared his baby brother had finally recognized the depth of his feelings for her, just in time to discover it was too late.

Cody met his gaze. "Will you explain to Daddy?"

"What do you want me to tell him?"

"Just that I had to get away."

"You will be back, though, right?"

Cody's gaze shifted away. "I don't think so. I think it's time I cut the ties to White Pines."

"But you love it here, more than any of us," Jordan protested, realizing at last the depths of Cody's despair. "It's in your blood."

"I know," he admitted, unshed tears visible in his eyes before he turned away to hide them. "Look, you can get out of here now. I'll be okay."

"I'm not leaving," Jordan insisted stubbornly. "Sleep on this. Maybe in the morning things will look different to you."

"Nothing will change," Cody declared grimly.

"Just give it until morning."

Cody tried to stare him down, but eventually he nodded. "If I do, you'll handle things with Daddy?"

Jordan heaved a sigh of resignation at the renewed note of determination he heard in his brother's voice. He knew in his gut that Cody wouldn't be swayed. Under the same circumstances, he probably wouldn't have been, either.

"I'll do my best," he promised. "On one condition."

Cody regarded him suspiciously. "What's that?"

"You'll tell us where you are. You won't cut yourself off from the family."

His brother nodded. "If you'll swear that none of you will ever tell Melissa where I am. I don't want to ever hear her pitiful excuses for what happened tonight. I don't ever want to see her again at all."

Jordan thought his brother was protesting a little too much, but he agreed. "We'll keep your whereabouts from her, if that's what you want. I'll see that the rest of the family agrees."

"Jessie, too?"

Jordan grinned. Their sister-in-law was a soft touch when it came to romance. "Jessie, too," he promised.

He bunked out on Cody's lumpy old sofa. Eventually he went to sleep, still praying that by morning his younger brother would come to his senses. No matter what he'd promised and would do if he had to, he really, really didn't want to be the one to explain to his father that Cody had taken off.

Harlan Adams had a tendency to fly off the handle and go after the messenger when he got bad news. This particular message was very likely to get him blasted with a shotgun.

Chapter Six

Cody was gone when Jordan awoke at daybreak. Obviously his brother had managed to find the truck keys in his pocket or he'd had a spare set hidden away that he'd forgotten about the night before in his fury over his girlfriend's betrayal.

Jordan groaned as he thought about what his father's reaction was going to be to the news. He worried, too, about whether Harlan could still handle all of the ranch's strenuous activities. As vital and fit as his father was, he had been depending more and more on Cody to run the day-to-day operations at White Pines. It was something that would have to be discussed, but to be perfectly honest, Jordan dreaded getting into it. His father hated even the slightest hint that Cody's role at White Pines had gradually become equal to or even more important than his own.

First things first, though. He had promised Kelly he'd be back this morning to offer more help with the fences. She'd probably be delighted if he failed to show, but he wasn't about to give her an excuse to accuse him of letting her down. Obviously she already had a lot she was blaming him for, garbage from their past he hadn't even been aware was simmering in her head. The workings of the female mind had always been a puzzle to him, except with Kelly. Now it appeared she was falling into that same incomprehensible pattern of behavior.

With some reluctance he reached for the phone and dialed the ranch. To his vague relief, Dani answered. At least with her, he wouldn't have to explain past actions.

"Hi, Jordan," she said so eagerly it made his heart flip over. "Thanks for the pizza. It was scrumpsi-delicious."

He grinned, despite his mood. "I'm glad you liked it."

"Did you and Mommy have a fight after I fell asleep in the car?" she asked, a frightened note in her voice. It was the concern of a child who'd already seen her father walk out of her life, no doubt after more than one angry exchange with her mother.

Jordan's heart thudded dully. How much could she possibly have heard? Why the devil hadn't they been more discreet? They'd both assumed that Dani was sleeping soundly in the back seat. "Why would you think that, munchkin?"

"Because Mommy looks all sad this morning and she yelled at me for watching a video instead of coming to take my bath."

So, Kelly looked sad, did she? He'd have to think about what that meant. As for her attitude toward Dani, he was pretty sure he wasn't the one responsible for that. "How many times had she called you to take your bath?"

"Once," Dani said.

Jordan had his doubts. "Really? Just once?"

"Maybe it was twice."

More likely double that, Jordan guessed. "Don't you think that could have had something to do with why she yelled?"

Dani sighed. "Maybe," she conceded. "She still looks sad, though. Are you coming over?"

"In a bit. Is your mom there?"

"She's in the shower."

The vivid image that appeared in Jordan's mind could have steamed up the whole state of Texas: Kelly naked, slick with water, her body provocatively covered with suds, his hands sliding slowly over her. He nearly moaned out loud, then caught himself. Thoughts like that about Kelly had never occurred to him in the past or, if they had, he had banished them at once. It was getting more and more difficult now to forget such images.

"Okay, munchkin, would you be sure to tell her I called?" He was proud of the steadiness of his voice when his pulse was still ricocheting wildly. "Tell her I have to spend some time with my father this morning, but I'll be there as soon as I can, okay? Can you remember that?''

''I can remember.''

''Tell her the minute she gets out of the shower.''

''Okay. 'Bye, Jordan.''

'' 'Bye, munchkin. See you later.''

Jordan left Cody's shortly after hanging up. The trip to the main house took only a few minutes, not nearly long enough for him to decide how to tell his father that Cody was gone. He didn't catch a break once he was there, either. He found Harlan already seated in the dining room, the newspaper spread open in front of him.

His father regarded him with open speculation as Jordan poured himself a cup of coffee and plucked a corn muffin he didn't really want off the buffet.

''You didn't listen to a word I said to you, did you?'' his father grumbled when Jordan was seated at the table.

''Which words of wisdom are you accusing me of ignoring?''

''You spent the night with that woman.''

He noticed that the note of glee in his father's voice contradicted the somewhat negative phrasing of the statement. It simply confirmed Jordan's suspicions that his father had been trying out a little reverse psychology on him by warning him away from Kelly.

''I assume you're referring to Kelly, and no, I did not spend the night with her,'' Jordan told him irritably, cutting the muffin into precise little sections to avoid having to meet his father's gaze. ''I was at Cody's.''

That grabbed his father's attention. Harlan's gaze narrowed suspiciously. "What the devil were you doing there?"

"Trying to persuade him not to hightail it away from here."

"Dammit all!" Harlan set his coffee cup down so hard, the coffee splattered all over the tablecloth. He made no attempt to blot it up. "Cody's leaving? Without a word to me? Damn that boy's hide."

"He's already left," Jordan corrected.

"Why would he want to go and do something crazy like that? We have work to do. He couldn't have picked a worse time for a vacation."

"I don't think he sees this as a vacation."

The color drained out of his father's face. "He's taken off for good?"

"So he claims."

He stared at Jordan, disbelief and anger warring on his face. "That's nuts," he protested. "He loves this place. It'll be his one day. You and Luke will get your shares, of course, but the ranch will belong to Cody."

"Which is exactly as it should be. He's the one who always wanted it."

"So, why the hell did he go and leave?" He waved his finger under Jordan's nose. "I'll tell you this, if he doesn't have a darn good explanation, I'll cut him out of my will, that's what I'll do."

His father's face was turning bright red as his anger mounted. Jordan suspected, though, that beneath that anger there was genuine concern. For all of his domineering attitude and his manipulations, Harlan loved his sons.

"Come on now, Daddy, settle down," he soothed. "You don't know the whole story."

"So tell me," his father snapped.

Jordan wasn't sure how much detail Cody would want him going into, but he realized his father wouldn't be satisfied with some evasive answer. "He and Melissa had some kind of a falling out. A pretty bad one. He needed to get his head straight, so he took off."

"To go where?"

"He didn't say. He did promise to let us know where he winds up on the condition that we never share that with Melissa. Who knows, maybe once he has time to cool off, he'll change his mind and come straight back here."

His father's shoulders sagged. "I always knew that boy was going to wake up too late and see what his fooling around and taking her for granted had cost him. Did she leave him for somebody else?"

Jordan refused to say. "I don't know that for sure." He studied his father worriedly. "Will you be okay around here? Have you got enough help?"

As he'd expected, Harlan immediately scowled at the question. "Boy, I was running this place when the whole bunch of you were in diapers. I suppose I'm capable of putting in a few more years of hard work."

"Luke would be willing to help out, I'm sure."

"He has his own place and his own family to think about." Harlan shook his head. "Dammit, Jordan, I don't want to tell your mama about this. This means some of those trips she has planned will have to be postponed. Besides that, she dotes on Cody. He was her baby."

Jordan wasn't sure there was much truth in that. He'd never noticed that his mother doted on anyone in the household except his father. Still, he asked, "Do you want me to tell her?"

"No, I'll do it." He leveled a hard gaze at Jordan. "There's just one thing I want to know, son. Why the hell didn't you do something to stop him? This thing with Melissa would have passed over quick enough, if he'd stayed here and dealt with it. Now who knows how long it'll fester inside him and keep him from coming home."

Jordan's own sense of guilt was as painful as any accusation his father could throw at him. "I did what I could," he said tersely. He stood. "You're sure you'll be okay?"

Harlan sighed. "I always am."

Despite the assurance, Jordan squeezed his father's shoulder on his way past. "I love you, old man."

His father's weathered, callused hand patted his. "I know you do, son."

"So does Cody."

His father nodded. "I know that, too." He glanced up. "You on your way back to Houston?"

"No. I'm going back over to Kelly's. She needs more help with that fence."

"Exactly how long will you be sticking around here, then?"

"That remains to be seen," Jordan said.

An awful lot depended on how long it took him to get Kelly to agree to his proposal. At some point in the past twenty-four hours he'd resolved not to leave until she said yes. Maybe it was Cody's reaction to losing Melissa, maybe it was his father's to Cody's departure, but suddenly he'd grasped that there was nothing more important on earth than family and he wanted to claim Kelly and Dani once and for all as his.

Kelly hadn't bothered the night before to tell Jordan that she and Dani always went to church on Sunday morning. She hadn't figured it mattered. He probably wouldn't show up anyway, not after the way she'd accused him of using her to fill in until the right woman came along. He'd appeared to be genuinely exasperated with her for reaching that conclusion. She couldn't imagine what else she was supposed to think, but he obviously resented the accusation.

At any rate, she wasn't all that surprised when he wasn't on her doorstep at dawn. All the way to church and back, she told herself it didn't matter, that she wasn't disappointed, that it would be better if he went back to Houston and got on with his life and let her get on with hers. She had too much pride to want to be a practice wife or a convenient hostess, until the right woman came along.

Apparently, however, that particular message didn't quite get from her brain to her traitorous heart. That blasted part of her anatomy reacted with pure delight when she spotted him rocking on her front porch as she drove up the lane to her house after church. She fought the impulse to race from the car and fling herself into his arms. Dani's reaction, however, was another thing entirely. For the first time Kelly could recall, her daughter didn't look overjoyed to see Jordan waiting on their doorstep.

"Uh-oh," Dani muttered, scooting down in the front seat.

Kelly glanced at her daughter and saw the worried frown puckering her brow. "What's wrong?"

"I forgot something."

Kelly glanced from Dani to Jordan and back again. "Something about Jordan?"

"Uh-huh."

A vague stirring of alarm spread through her. "What did you forget?"

"He called before."

"Jordan called?" She had to battle with herself to keep her voice from climbing. There was no point in letting her daughter know how much that small, seemingly inconsequential piece of information meant to her. "When?"

"When you were in the shower," Dani admitted in a tiny voice. "He said he had to go see his father and he'd be here later."

"Did you tell him we were going to church?"

Dani shook her head. "I'm sorry, Mommy. He made me promise to tell you, but I just forgot. Don't be mad at me."

Kelly reached over and rubbed her daughter's cheek with her knuckles. How could she not forgive her? Dani didn't have a mean-spirited bone in her body.

And she was obviously contrite. There was, however, a lesson to be learned here.

"I'm not mad," she reassured her. "But Jordan is another matter. You made a promise to him and you didn't keep it. How do you propose to handle it?"

Blue eyes, filled with dismay, gazed up at her. "I have to 'pologize, huh?"

"I'd say so."

"Is he going to be really, really mad?"

"Oh, I think Jordan is a fair man. He'll listen to what you have to say. Go on, now. Run and tell him what happened."

With obvious reluctance, Dani unhooked her seat belt and slipped out of the car. Kelly hid a grin as she watched her daughter crossing the yard, her gaze fixed on Jordan. No criminal heading for the hanging tree had ever walked at a more halting pace. She paused at the bottom of the steps. From the car, Kelly could hear her hesitant greeting.

Jordan's rocker stilled as he listened to the stammered apology. Kelly slowly left the car and went to join them. As she approached, she didn't dare risk a glance into his eyes for fear they'd both start chuckling.

"I see," he said quietly when Dani concluded her explanation for breaking her promise. "Will it ever happen again?"

Dani shook her head emphatically. "Never. I really, really promise. Cross my heart. Next time I'll even write it down, if you'll show me how to spell your name."

Jordan held out his hand. "Then that's good enough for me. Apology accepted. And I'll teach you to spell my name later on this afternoon."

Relief spreading across her face, Dani bolted up the stairs and flung herself into Jordan's arms. After a startled look at Kelly, he picked the child up and hugged her. A wistful expression passed across his face as Dani's arms wound tightly around his neck.

In that instant, watching the two of them with a lump in her throat, something inside Kelly shifted. Suddenly she began to envision possibilities that she'd been staunchly denying for weeks now. If Jordan could accept Dani as his own, if he could love her child as she did, then perhaps his feelings for her didn't really matter. If she could guarantee Dani's happiness by giving her a father, then perhaps she could live with no more than Jordan's affection for herself.

"So, where have you two been?" Jordan inquired after Dani disentangled herself and received permission to go to the barn to check on the kittens as soon as she'd changed her clothes.

Kelly propped herself against the porch rail. "Church."

"You didn't mention anything about that yesterday when I told you I'd be back this morning to help with the fences."

Kelly shrugged. "We've always gone to church on Sunday, before doing any work. Besides, I thought you'd probably change your mind."

"Because?"

"Because of last night."

He nodded slowly. "I'll admit what you said in the car took me by surprise. It never occurred to me that you would think I intended our marriage to be anything less than the real thing. That's not the way I do business."

Kelly frowned. "Business?"

He had the good grace to wince. "Sorry. Force of habit. I spend an awful lot of time negotiating deals. The terminology is ingrained."

She tried to cling to the pragmatic way she'd felt only moments ago, but his attitude grated. She couldn't help it. She didn't like being viewed as part of a business deal, something acquired with no more emotion than he might display when gobbling up a new company for his corporation. Maybe marrying Jordan for Dani's sake wouldn't be so smart, after all. She'd have to think about it long and hard, far longer than it appeared he was inclined to give her.

"I'm going in to change," she said, heading for the door.

"Kelly?"

"Drop it for now, Jordan." Still holding the screen door open, she glanced back at him. There was an oddly forlorn expression on his face she didn't know how to interpret. "Stay for Sunday dinner, if you like. We'll work afterward."

He brightened at once. "Fried chicken?"

She grinned at his enthusiasm. The way to this man's heart had always been through his stomach, no doubt about it. "Always," she assured him.

"You know something?"

"What?"

"It's really good to know that some things never change. Fried chicken on Sundays is one." He paused, his gaze fixed on her. "You're another. Please don't ever go and change on me, Kelly."

She thought about that remark the whole time she was changing clothes. A few minutes later she met Jordan in the kitchen. He was already setting the table for her, just as he had whenever her mother had invited him to stay for Sunday dinner years ago. He'd even taken out the good china, just as he'd been instructed to do back then.

"Another old habit?" she teased.

"Exactly." His gaze settled on her. "It feels right being here, Kelly."

She nodded, unable to say anything. Having him here felt too darned right to her, too. It was a dangerous sensation, a trap she didn't dare fall into. Nostalgia was no reason to get married.

Getting a grip on her emotions, she put him to work peeling potatoes next. As she prepared the chicken, she watched him closely. Despite his expressed contentment at being there, there was something quiet and distant about him that was out of character.

"Jordan, what's going on with you?" she asked eventually.

He glanced up from the mound of potatoes forming in front of him. "It's Cody."

Kelly's heart thumped unsteadily as she imagined the youngest of the brothers injured or worse. She'd been gone when Erik was killed in an accident on Luke's ranch, but she'd spent time with Jordan after that and seen how devastating it had been for him. It hadn't been easy for her, either. She'd felt as if she'd lost her own brother. If something had happened to sweet, irrepressible Cody... She didn't even want to think about it.

"Has something happened to Cody?"

Apparently he heard the alarm in her voice, because he reached out and touched her hand.

"Nothing like that," he reassured her hurriedly. He went on to tell her about Cody's abrupt departure the night before. "Daddy's fit to be tied, not just at Cody, but at me for not stopping him."

Kelly could just imagine the guilt trip Harlan was capable of laying on Jordan. "Cody's a grown man. He has to handle his problems whatever way works for him. I could shake Melissa, though, for doing something like that. It doesn't make any sense. She's adored Cody forever."

"That's what I thought, but Cody swears he saw what he saw. He couldn't wait to take off. Now Daddy's threatening to cut him out of the will. Whatever he feels right now, it would kill Cody to lose White Pines."

"Would Harlan really disinherit him?"

"I suppose that depends on how long Cody stays away. You know how stubborn Daddy is."

Kelly surveyed him pointedly. "I certainly do. It's a trait he passed along to all of you."

"I'm not stubborn," Jordan denied.

"Oh, please."

"Determined, maybe. Dedicated."

"Bullheaded," she corrected.

He grinned, that lopsided, boyish grin that was so at odds with the sophisticated image he'd projected in recent years. "If you know that, then you should know you haven't got a chance in fighting me on this proposal."

"You're forgetting one thing."

"Which is?"

"I am every bit as bullheaded as you are, Jordan Adams."

"Admittedly a frightening thought," he teased. "But you don't scare me, Kelly Flint. You're weakening already. I can tell."

Kelly swallowed hard against the tide of pure panic that his observation sent through her. "How can you tell a thing like that?"

"Oh, no, you don't. I'm not telling you my secret way of figuring out what's really going on in that head of yours. It's the only advantage I've got."

It wasn't, Kelly thought with a sigh. The real advantage he had was that she was still head over heels in love with him.

Chapter Seven

Kelly spent the rest of the day watching as the bond between her daughter and Jordan miraculously strengthened. It was as if some barrier inside Jordan had fallen and allowed him to open his heart to the child. Always stiff, formal and a little aloof in the past, today he had finally relaxed, reminding her why she had wanted him as Dani's godfather in the first place. Well, one of the reasons, anyway.

To her initial surprise Paul had been delighted with the choice. An ambitious man, she finally realized that he relished the tie to the powerful Jordan Adams. Kelly could hardly criticize his motives, when her own were less than pure. She had asked Jordan to be Dani's godfather, not only because he was the sort of stable, bright, fun-loving influence she wanted for her child, but because it would forever link them all together.

Jordan had balked at first, swearing that what he knew about children would fit on the head of a pin. Kelly had had to use every persuasive skill at her command to talk him into it.

Now, observing the two of them, she was glad she had. Just seeing their heads close together as Jordan tried to teach Dani how to make homemade peach ice cream after they'd worked on the fence for awhile made Kelly's resolve slip another notch. Soon she wouldn't have any reserves of willpower left for resisting him. Dani wanted a father desperately and Jordan was slowly but surely slipping into that role. It was far more natural to him than he had once insisted or she had once imagined.

She closed her eyes against the sight of man and child, but she couldn't stop her thoughts from dashing headlong back to a time when she'd dreamed of seeing Jordan with their child in just such a scene. She'd envisioned a pint-size boy, his thick, sun-streaked hair falling in his face, wearing tiny cowboy boots and trailing after his daddy with the same rolling cowboy gait. She'd imagined a little girl with dark brown curls and big brown eyes cuddled in her father's arms as he rocked her to sleep, crooning a lullaby in his deep, soothing voice.

Dani's excited shouts cut into her reverie.

"Mommy, I did it!" Dani hollered, thundering onto the porch, a bowl in her hand. "Look! I made ice cream!"

It looked more like soup to Kelly, but she didn't complain as she took the offered bowl and tried a taste. "Wonderful," she declared. "The best peach ice cream I've ever had. Maybe you two will turn out to be the next ice cream magnates."

"Peach is good, but chocolate is better. Jordan says next time we'll make that. It's his favorite, too."

"Oh, really? You and Jordan seem to be making a lot of plans today."

Jordan strolled up to the porch and leaned back against the railing right smack in front of her, a position that put his incredible thighs and other interesting parts of his anatomy practically at eye level. Kelly jerked her gaze up to rest more safely on his face. He shot her a knowing little grin that set her teeth on edge.

"Any objections to our plans?" he inquired, clearly daring her to challenge his determination to weave himself into the fabric of their lives.

Kelly waited until Dani had scampered off to check the ice-cream maker before responding. "Only if you intend to disappoint her," she warned in a low voice. "Paul has done enough of that to last her a lifetime."

"I will never disappoint her or you," he vowed, regarding her solemnly. "You can take that promise to the bank."

As soon as the businesslike words were out of his mouth, he looked chagrined. "Sorry."

"I know, force of habit."

Somehow, though, this time she couldn't work herself into much of a snit over it. With the sun setting into a purple haze of twilight and the fragrance of flowers filling the hot, dry air, she felt too at ease, too comfortable with the camaraderie they'd shared all day long to risk spoiling it with another quarrel over semantics. Jordan would probably always use business terms for describing things. At least he'd formally asked her to marry him, not to enter into a merger.

Besides, it was getting late, too late to squabble and ruin an otherwise perfect day. It was time for Dani to be going to bed and soon it would be time for Jordan to be going back to Houston. She was surprised he'd hung around this long. By Sunday evenings he was usually chomping at the bit to get away from west Texas and back to the big city so he could dig into the piles of work he always brought home from the office.

"You leaving for Houston soon?" she asked.

"Trying to get rid of me?"

"No, just wondering."

"I'm not going back."

Startled, she stared at him. "You mean tonight?"

"I mean, not until you and I reach some sort of compromise."

She knew what compromise meant in Jordan's terms. He wanted her to capitulate completely. She shot him a wry look. "It's a little early for you to think about retiring over here to wait me out."

"Oh, I don't anticipate it taking nearly that long."

After glancing to make sure that Dani was occupied and out of hearing range, Kelly warned him emphatically, "You will not bully me into making a decision."

He shrugged, looking supremely confident. "I didn't plan to."

She sighed. "You're just going to try to wear me down, then, aren't you?"

"I prefer to think of it as winning you over to my way of thinking."

Before she could respond to that, Dani rejoined them, leaning against Kelly's thigh and yawning widely. "Sleepy?" Kelly asked, looping an arm around the child's waist and hugging her close.

"Uh-huh," she admitted.

"Then run up and fill the tub. I'll be up in a minute to give you your bath and tuck you in."

"But I just took a bath before church."

"And you got filthy again today."

"Okay." Dani gazed sleepily up at Jordan. "Will you stay and read me a story?" she asked, an unmistakable wistful note in her voice.

Kelly saw the hesitancy in Jordan's eyes and silently cursed him. Before she could jump in, though, he grinned. "You have anything with horses in it?"

Dani beamed. "*Black Beauty.* It's my favorite."

"Ah, yes, I think I remember that one. It was your mom's favorite, too."

Kelly stared at him. "How on earth do you remember that?"

"There's a lot I remember about you," he taunted. "For a very long time you told me all your deepest, darkest secrets. For instance—"

The devilish twinkle in his eyes caused Kelly to cut him off. There was no telling what story he'd share with her daughter, if she didn't watch her step. "Never mind," she said in a rush. "If you don't mind staying around to read, the bath shouldn't take more than fifteen minutes or so."

"I'll clean up the ice-cream maker." He caught her gaze. "Maybe I'll bunk out on your sofa tonight, so we can get an early start on those fences in the morning."

"You're thinking of staying here?" she repeated weakly.

"Do you have a problem with that?"

She had a problem with it, all right, but it wasn't one she intended to share with him. She simply shook her head and fled inside with her daughter.

As she was bathing Dani, she couldn't help hearing Jordan moving around downstairs. Just knowing he was in the house made her feel different somehow, protected, warmed. Heck, who was she kidding? She felt a shivery stirring of anticipation knowing that he intended to stay the night. He'd suggested the sofa, but there was a perfectly good guest room right next to her own and he well knew it. She would be able to imagine him in that bed, perhaps even hear the steady rhythm of his breathing. The very thought tantalized her.

Sure, they'd all camped out together as kids, with his father or hers along as a chaperon for the whole rowdy bunch of them, but this was different. This meant spending the night under the same roof with a man who claimed to want her as his wife, a man she'd wanted in her bed since she'd first discovered the chemistry at work between a man and a woman.

The thought of testing that chemistry intrigued her, until she realized that would make her no better than Jordan. She had accused him of wanting a practice wife. Surely she shouldn't be considering testing their relationship to see if the chemistry was right between them.

Besides, for her part, she knew it was. She'd been going weak in the knees around Jordan too many years not to know it. As for him, he was too much a sexual being to want to marry her if he didn't intend to sleep with her. That must mean that he found her attractive. In fact, she thought she'd even detected a smoldering look of desire in his eyes on more than one occasion lately, especially when he'd watched her face as he'd displayed all that sexy lingerie he'd bought her.

A timely splash of cool water hit her square in the face.

"Mommy, you're not paying attention to me," Dani accused. "I could drown."

"Who are you kidding? You can swim like a fish."

"Not in the tub," Dani declared. "Am I clean yet? I want to go hear *Black Beauty.*"

"I suppose you're clean enough," Kelly agreed, holding open a towel and folding her daughter into it and rubbing her briskly. She picked up a blue-and-white cotton Dallas Cowboys T-shirt that was Dani's favorite sleepwear. "Put this on and then hop into bed. I'll get Jordan."

She opened the bathroom door and practically tripped over his booted feet. "Jordan!"

"Thought I'd save you the trip down to get me."

"How thoughtful!"

He grinned unrepentantly as he followed her to Dani's room. "By the way, I like the decor."

Kelly glanced around at the Winnie the Pooh wallpaper and stuffed animal collection that filled half a dozen shelves. "Somehow this doesn't strike me as you."

"I was referring to your room."

Her gaze shot up. Her pulse skittered crazily. "You were in my room?"

"The door was open. I peeked." He rocked back on his heels. "Expecting company?"

Hands on her hips, Kelly glared at him. "What is that supposed to mean? Any company I have stays in the guest room. And," she added pointedly, "that includes you."

"But that king-size bed is really something. Doesn't it get lonely?"

She continued to scowl and said pointedly, "It hasn't yet."

"Liar," he whispered in her ear just as Dani came bounding in and plucked her book from the shelves. She thrust it into Jordan's hands.

"Read," she ordered imperiously.

"My pleasure," he told her, but his gaze was still fixed firmly on Kelly's blushing face. Apparently satisfied that he'd completely disconcerted her, he settled down onto a chair beside the bed and dutifully began to read.

Kelly stared at him and at her daughter. Dani was obviously enraptured by the dramatic telling of her favorite story. She sighed. She wished a bedtime story were all she wanted from Jordan. She wanted more than that, though, much more. And very little of what she hungered for was nearly so innocent as a bedtime story.

And every time he snuck beneath or over or around her defenses, she wanted it all with a desperation that stunned her. Not sure she could bear it another minute, she slipped from Dani's bedroom and retreated downstairs.

Away from him, away from the two of them, she struggled to get her bearings. Unfortunately, she suspected that there weren't enough hours in the day or weeks in the year for her to ever build up adequate resistance to the man upstairs.

Jordan found Kelly in the kitchen an hour later, stirring her cup of tea distractedly, even though he knew perfectly well she had put neither sugar nor cream nor lemon in it. Nervous habit, he guessed, and hid a smile.

He noticed she'd swept her hair up off her neck into a loose ponytail. Escaping tendrils curled softly against her skin. Suddenly he wanted very badly to press a kiss to that tender spot on the back of her neck. He weighed his desire against the temperature of that steaming cup of tea she was likely to heave at him and decided against it. He still had to go slowly here or lose what little ground he had gained with her.

He poured himself a cup of tea from the pot on the table and took a seat next to her. Beneath the table, their thighs brushed. Alarm sparked in her eyes, but he knew she had too much pride to let him know he was getting to her. Aside from the sudden rigidity of her posture, she gave no other hint of how desperately she wanted to flee. Those delectable, stiff little shoulders told him he was on the right track, though. From now on he intended to crowd her a bit, literally and figuratively.

"Is Dani asleep?" she asked.

He noticed the thready huskiness in her voice. It confirmed that the tactic was working. She was not nearly as immune to him as she wanted to pretend. Of course, being this close to her without sweeping her into his arms was also killing him, but it was a torture he was willing to endure if it accomplished his goal.

"She's out like a light," he confirmed. "I was so caught up in the story, I read all the way to the end of the chapter before I noticed."

"I could loan you the book," Kelly offered, amusement dancing in her eyes.

"I think I'll just stick around for a while and finish it here."

"Jordan . . ." She sighed and fell silent, the protest left incomplete.

"Go on, say it," he urged. "We can't settle this, if we aren't open and honest."

He saw the familiar quick temper flare in her eyes again.

"This is not a damned business negotiation," she reminded him for the umpteenth time. She held up her hands. "Never mind. I don't want to talk about this again anyway."

Jordan caught one of her hands in midair and lifted it to his lips. The kiss clearly caught her off guard. Her gaze shot to his and she struggled to yank her hand away. He held on for one more soft brush of his lips over her knuckles. Despite the gloves she wore for work, there were tiny nicks scattered across that pale skin. He touched his mouth to every one. He could feel her pulse scamper wildly. Her hand in his trembled. He finally took pity on her and released the hand.

"What are you doing?" she demanded indignantly. She shoved both hands under the table out of view, but, as they both knew, hardly out of reach.

He chuckled. "You're not that naive."

"No, I'm not," she snapped. "Which is why I want to know what you're up to."

"No secret there. I'm trying to get you to marry me. I'll use most any means I have to, fair or foul, to persuade you. I am willing to compromise, though, on certain points," he said, deliberately using the business terminology he knew she hated. Predictable fire danced in her eyes.

"Compromise?" she repeated, her tone ominous.

"Of course. I'm a reasonable man." He was pleased with himself for having thought of this, to say nothing of feeling downright noble.

"And what exactly are you willing to compromise about?"

"For starters, you hate Houston. I hate ranch life."
The last was an understatement, which made his
willingness to reach a middle ground all the more in-
dicative of how serious he was about this. Kelly had
listened to him ranting and raving about getting away
from west Texas for years before he'd finally gone.
She had to know how significant this particular compromise was for him.

"True. What do you suggest?" Kelly asked, regarding him doubtfully. "That we move to Bos-
ton?"

She sounded testy. He figured that was because she
knew she couldn't argue with his logic. "Don't be
absurd," he chided. "We'll commute. Weekdays in
Houston. Weekends, holidays and vacations on the
ranch."

She didn't look nearly as bowled over by the proposed arrangement as he'd hoped.

"Uh-huh. And who is supposed to work the ranch
while I'm in Houston?"

He hadn't considered all the details, but he'd
learned long ago to be quick on his feet in a discussion of this importance. "You have a hand working
for you already. We'll hire an experienced foreman."

"I can't afford to hire someone."

Jordan was getting a headache. Clearly Kelly didn't
know the meaning of the word compromise. She
wasn't shifting her position by so much as an inch as
near as he could tell. "But I can."

She was already shaking her head. "I promised
myself that I would make a go of the ranch on my
own," she insisted.

"Why does it have to be totally on your own? Why can't you accept a little help?"

"Because it's my fault it's in the state it's in," she snapped, then looked shocked by what she'd revealed.

"Why on earth would you think you're to blame?"

"Because if I'd stayed here and helped out instead of running off to Houston, things would never have gotten this bad."

"That's ridiculous," he declared. "Besides, that's all in the past. Let's deal with the here and now."

"Okay," she said agreeably. "Maybe by next year I could afford help, but not now. That's the reality of the here and now."

The woman was stubborn as a mule. He wondered if she'd been born that way or if she'd picked it up from hanging around with him and his brothers. Goodness knew, they all had stubbornness to spare.

"Oh, for pity's sake," he snapped impatiently. "I'll loan you the money."

"No bank would take a risk on me," she countered coolly. "Why should you?"

"Because it's the only way I know to get you to budge from this place," he said, thoroughly exasperated.

There were moments—and now was definitely one of them—when he thought he might have been deranged to suggest this whole marriage idea. He and Kelly hadn't had a quiet, serene exchange in weeks. He hadn't had a decent night's sleep.

And too damned many of his waking moments he'd been rock-hard just thinking about her. He supposed that feeling passion for the woman he'd decided to marry was a good thing. It was just that it had come about so unexpectedly. One minute he'd been planning to lead a nice, tame existence with a safe, uncomplicated pal, a woman who shared his values and his history. The next he hadn't been able to stop thinking about seducing her, about running his hands over her body, about the taste of her lips, the shape of her breasts, the texture of her skin.

He groaned. Talk about complications! If he so much as looked at her tonight, he was liable to make love to her here and now, on top of the kitchen table. His decision to crowd her had clearly backfired. He was the one in turmoil, while she looked calm as could be.

He shoved his chair back from the table and abruptly stood. "I have to go," he said, his voice choked, his gaze very carefully averted.

"I thought you were going to spend the night here."

On the sofa? Or, as she had suggested, in the guest room? Less than thirty feet from that king-size bed of hers? Not if there was an armed posse surrounding the place and he was the target. He bolted for the door, not certain exactly where he was headed. He wasn't sure he was up to one of his father's inquisitions about Cody.

"I'm going to stay with Luke and Jessie," he announced. The drive to their place ought to be just about long enough to cool him off and it would keep him out of range of his father's anger for another night.

Kelly didn't offer another protest. Oddly enough, he thought he caught the faintest hint of a smile right before she closed the door behind him. He had the feeling he didn't want to know what *that* had been about.

Chapter Eight

"Ginger, I want you to cancel all my meetings for the rest of the week," Jordan told his secretary when he called Houston first thing on Monday morning. It was only 8:00 a.m., but he knew she'd already been at her desk for at least half an hour. Most of the time she even beat him to the office and he was an early starter.

"You're going on your honeymoon," she guessed, sounding far more pleased than she had when he'd told her about his engagement to Rexanne. "You must have finally talked Kelly into getting married. Congratulations, boss!"

"I wish," he said dully.

"She hasn't said yes yet?"

The shock in Ginger's voice gave him some encouragement. Obviously she thought he was a catch, even if Kelly did not. "Not even maybe," he admitted.

"Well, for heaven's sake, boss, you can't just shut down business on a whim. How long do you expect it to take to persuade her?"

"You're a woman. You tell me."

"Did you do like I said? Did you buy some of that French perfume? Did you tell her you loved her?"

Jordan supposed his silence was answer enough, because Ginger gave a little snort of disgust. "Jeez, boss, you're missing the most obvious things. Perfume is equated with sex, at least the right one is. And every woman wants the man she's marrying to be crazy in love with her. Stop being so stodgy and do something over the top for a change. Dazzle her."

"But this is Kelly," he protested. "We've known each other forever. She doesn't expect all that hearts and flowers sentiment. She'd probably laugh in my face."

Ginger sighed heavily. "Boss, I hate to say it, but you deserve to remain single. You might as well come on back to Houston now, because if Kelly has a brain in her head, which she obviously does, she'll boot you out of there sooner or later anyway. You'll wind up with one of those dull, grasping socialites, who won't care how you woo them as long as you ultimately give them access to your bank account."

"Thanks for the vote of confidence," he said, thoroughly demoralized. "Just cancel the meetings, okay? Or see if one of the others can take them. Mark could probably handle the one with the equipment manufacturer." He listed others that could be turned over to key members of his staff. "You'll have to postpone the rest."

"And what am I supposed to tell people?"

"Tell them I'm working on a major acquisition and it's taking more of my time than I'd planned."

Ginger gave another derisive sniff. "Tell Kelly that, why don't you? That'll really win her over."

Jordan wasn't about to admit to her that his lack of romanticism was already a major bone of contention between Kelly and him. "Just do what I asked, please. I'll see you next week."

"Bet it'll be sooner," Ginger muttered.

"Goodbye," he said pointedly. "Call me at Kelly's if you need me."

"I think maybe I'll try reaching you at White Pines first. Odds are that's where you'll be."

She hung up before he could respond to her final, stinging taunt. Damn, what was with women, anyway? They all stuck together. He suspected Jessie would be no different.

Now that he thought about it, maybe that was the real reason he'd driven all the way to Luke's the night before. He'd wanted a chance to test his thinking on his brother's wife.

Jessie had always struck him as a sweet, practical, no-nonsense kind of woman. She was very fond of Kelly. Surely she would see the sense in the arrangement he was proposing to Kelly. Like him, Jessie would want what was best for her friend. Someone who would look after her and Dani.

He found Jessie downstairs in the kitchen. The baby was propped up in her high chair and Jessie was spooning something that looked like watered-down oatmeal into her mouth. Most of it appeared to be on Angela's face and the floor with a goodly portion streaked from Jessie's face all the way down the front of her blouse. Oddly enough, she didn't seem to mind.

The minute Jessie spotted him, she stood and shoved the tiny spoon into his hand. "Feed her, would you? I need to check the laundry."

"Can't she wait?" he inquired, staring helplessly from Jessie to the baby and back again. Before the words were out of his mouth, Angela balled her tiny hands into fists and began whimpering. Jessie didn't even glance back.

"Okay, okay," he murmured, taking a seat opposite the baby. He dipped the spoon into the cereal, if that's what it was, and aimed at Angela's mouth. Unfortunately the target moved. The cereal dribbled down her cheek. She seemed pleased, though, that he'd tried. She smiled happily, displaying what might have been the beginnings of a tooth.

"Let's try this again," he said, bolstered by that smile. The next spoonful actually made it into her mouth, then dribbled out. He had the strangest suspicion that this was a game she enjoyed playing. Another perverse woman in the making, he decided with a sigh of resignation.

He scooped up more of the disgusting cereal and aimed again. This time she hit the spoon and splattered it back on him. Globs of the white stuff stuck to his shirt. He was forced to admit to a certain admiration for her muscle tone. She'd whacked that spoon with real strength.

Babies were obviously more of a challenge than he'd originally thought. He made up his mind to get the hang of dealing with them. After all, he supposed that sooner or later he and Kelly would want children of their own, baby brothers and sisters for Dani. He hadn't given a lot of consideration to kids in the past, but his experiences with Dani lately were changing his mind.

"Do you really want this stuff?" he inquired. "Frankly, it looks pretty disgusting to me."

"You're not the one eating it," Jessie retorted, coming back from the laundry room just in time to hear him trying to get out of feeding her child. She glanced at his shirt. "Maybe I'd better put that in with the next load of laundry."

"Do you do one after every meal?" he inquired, glancing around at the diaper she'd used to mop up previous spills, at Angela's filthy romper and Jessie's own spotted clothes.

"Actually, I've threatened to wear a plastic garbage bag with a slit in the top for my head," she admitted. "It's not always this bad, though." She grinned. "And sometimes it's much worse. Spinach is the pits."

"How reassuring. No wonder Luke has taken a powder and left you in charge."

"He's been gone since sunrise. He swears it's because there's work to be done, but I have my doubts. I think you may be right. He took one look at his precious daughter after her first experiment with baby food and decided not to show up for mealtime until she reaches her teens. He has this illusion that she's perfect and perfect does not include this particular image."

Jordan heard the tolerant amusement in her voice and saw the sparkle in her eyes. There was no mistaking the love radiating from her when she talked about her baby or his brother. He wondered if he and Kelly would ever have that kind of emotion between them. Probably not the way he was going about things, he was forced to admit. Ginger might have a point about that, though he'd sure as hell never tell her that. She was impossible enough as it was.

"Can I ask you a question?"

"Sure," Jessie said as she carefully spooned the remaining cereal into Angela's mouth. "Does it have something to do with Kelly?"

He wasn't all that surprised that she'd guessed. Harlan had probably mentioned his suspicions to Luke. Or, more likely, Kelly had told Jessie herself. He knew they talked regularly.

"What did she tell you?" he asked.

"About?" she replied noncommittally.

"Us."

Jessie spared him a glance. "Us? As in you and Kelly?"

"You don't have to act so innocent. I'm sure she told you I'd proposed."

Her expression turned quizzical. "Is that what it was?"

Jordan moaned. "Not you, too?"

"Well, you have to admit your technique lacked finesse."

"I sent flowers. I had a message flown over the ranch. I had thousands of rose petals dropped from the sky. I brought her sexy lingerie. The stuff damned near drove me wild imagining her in it. She didn't even take it out of the box."

Jessie's eyes widened at the mention of the lingerie. "Oh, really? She didn't mention that."

Jordan thought of how embarrassed Kelly had been by that particular gift. "I'm not surprised." He stared at Jessie, feeling totally bemused and helpless for the first time in his life. He didn't like the sensation at all. "I even offered to compromise on where we live."

Jessie put aside the bowl of cereal and leveled a penetrating look straight at him. "Before I answer, may I ask you a question?"

"Of course."

"Do you love her?"

Ginger had essentially asked the same thing and he'd been unwilling or unable to answer. He saw that he couldn't evade Jessie so easily. He had the feeling she could read between the lines of whatever answer he chose to give.

"I don't know what I feel," he admitted candidly. "She's always been a part of my life. I never thought of her in any way other than the best friend I ever had until recently."

"After your engagement to that awful Rexanne person fell apart?"

Another vote weighed in against his ex-fiancée. He must have been blind. "Exactly," he said.

"So you decided to rebound straight to the woman who'd been the one safe, secure constant in your life."

It didn't sound nearly so sensible or laudable when Jessie described it. "Something like that."

"She ought to knock your teeth down your throat," Jessie said succinctly.

His eyes widened. "Thanks."

"I'm serious. Of all the selfish, pigheaded decisions, Jordan Adams, that takes the cake. I'd say you'd better think long and hard about what you really want out of this relationship before you push Kelly's back to the wall. She's my friend and I don't want to see her hurt again. If you can't admit you love her, I'll stand up and shout my objections right smack in the middle of the service when the preacher asks if anyone knows just cause why you shouldn't be wed. I guarantee I'll make it the most humiliating moment of your life."

He saw evidence of the fiery temper Luke had mentioned on occasion, but no one else had ever seen in calm, serene Jessie. "You would, wouldn't you?" he said in amazement.

"Damn straight."

He grinned despite himself. "I'm glad she has you for a friend." He stood and headed for the door. "Fair warning, though. If I ever do manage to convince her to marry me, I may put a muzzle on you before I let you near the church."

Jessie didn't even flinch. "Tell her you love her and you won't have to."

The words echoed in his head all the way back to Kelly's ranch. After stopping in town to buy a picnic lunch, he sped the rest of the way to her house. He parked beside her car, checked the house for her even though he knew it was unlikely she'd be there in the middle of the day, then saddled up a horse and rode off in search of her.

As he rode, with the sun beating down on his shoulders and fluffy white clouds scudding across the vivid blue sky, he tried to analyze why he was so determined to marry Kelly. Was it pure cussedness because she'd said no and no one ever turned down Jordan Adams? Or was it something more, some feeling deep inside he'd never before analyzed too closely? Had all those times he'd gravitated to her house, ostensibly just to check up on her, been indications that she fulfilled some need in him?

He looked to his own parents for some clue about what love was all about. Harlan and Mary Adams had been married nearly thirty-five years. His father's eyes still shone whenever his wife walked into a room. As for his mother, she wasn't an especially warm woman, except when it came to her husband. With him, she radiated charm and laughter and the heat of desire even after all these years. They shared common goals and an abiding affection. Their marriage had been an example to all of their sons, even if Mary Adams's parenting skills had left something to be desired.

Surely, he thought, he and Kelly felt some of those same things. Maybe he'd just never put a label to them before. Maybe he'd repeatedly come back to west Texas, back to her, because he knew that with her he felt whole as he did with no one else on earth. Was that love?

He'd called himself in love with Rexanne and with others before her. He'd tacked the label on his feelings, because it seemed to be expected. But whatever emotions he'd felt then now seemed pale in comparison to the depth of what he felt when he was with Kelly and with Dani. He felt passion with Kelly, but he also felt a rare contentment, the kind that would endure. It was that, he knew, that had drawn him back to her.

Maybe he could say he loved her and say it in all honesty. Damn, but it was complicated, though. He didn't want to lie to her about something this important. He didn't want her to marry him under false pretenses. He'd been fooled before by love. So had she. He didn't want to make a mistake like that again, especially not with Kelly. She deserved only words he could back up with total conviction. One man like Paul Flint was more than any woman deserved.

It would be easy enough to say what she expected, to utter those three little words that would end this stalemate, but would it be fair? Would it be honest, when he was filled with so many doubts and questions?

He resolved to his regret that it would not be. If she accepted his proposal, it would have to be with the understanding that his feelings were still unclear, even to him. She would have to say *yes* knowing that while the commitment was as solid as granite, his emotions were more like quicksand, riddled with uncertainty.

He spotted her off in the distance just then, the sun glistening off her hair, the hat she wore only under duress dangling around her neck. Dani was seated on the saddle in front of her, a tiny cowboy hat perched on her head, her short legs clinging to the sides of the horse. Something inside him melted at the sight of them. If what he felt wasn't love, it was something darned close to it.

Dani saw him first and waved. "Hi, Jordan," she shouted, the greeting carrying on the still, hot, dry air.

Kelly's head snapped up. She was obviously startled to see him riding toward them. "I thought you'd be long gone by now," she said when he neared.

There was an uneasiness in her eyes that he deeply regretted. He knew he'd put it there with all of his pushing. Yet he knew this was too critical to their future for him to back off.

"I still have a very important matter pending," he said, his gaze even with hers and unrelenting.

She seemed to squeeze Dani a little more tightly against her body, the protective instinct of a mother with her endangered child. Or was it the mother who felt endangered in this instance?

"Jordan, this isn't the time," she said briskly, warning him to silence with a glance at Dani, then adding pointedly, "I have work to do."

"And I'll help," he promised. "But you have to break for lunch sometime. Why not now? I see the perfect spot over there under that old cottonwood." He gestured toward the basket he'd filled with sandwiches and ice-cold lemonade. "I brought a picnic."

"With potato salad?" Dani asked, oblivious to the undercurrents between the two adults. "And peanut butter and jelly?"

"You bet," he said, relieved that he'd thought of a child's tastes and included the peanut butter and jelly. "Cookies, too."

Kelly shook her head. "At this rate, you're going to win by default," she accused, relenting and turning her horse toward the shady spot to the west. "The ranch will fall apart because the work's not getting done, then where will I be?"

"You'll always have a place with me." He gazed directly into Kelly's eyes again as he set Dani down and sent her off to unpack the picnic basket. "Would it be so awful?" he asked when Dani was out of hearing.

A glint of determination flashed in her eyes. "Under those circumstances? Yes," she said without hesitation. "I told you that fixing this place up is important to me."

Jordan couldn't help admiring the streak of pride that kept her focused on making a go of this ranch entirely on her own, even if it was making his task a whole lot harder. "Then I'll just have to help ensure that it doesn't fall apart, won't I?"

She frowned. "We've been over this already. I won't take your money, Jordan."

"How about my help?" he retorted softly.

She hesitated, then sighed. "No rancher ever turns down an offer of help," she said. "As long as there are no strings attached."

"No strings," he assured her. Just when she appeared to relax slightly, he added, "For now."

Kelly was losing the battle. Every time she turned around all week long, Jordan was there, offering support, muscle and laughter. Every night Dani crawled into his lap after dinner and begged to be told a story about when he and her mother were little like her. Jordan seemed to enjoy the reminiscing almost as much as Dani did.

Even the old tomcat had turned traitor. He'd taken to curling up at Jordan's feet, purring loudly whenever Jordan deigned to rub his stomach.

More often than not, though, his gaze would cut to Kelly, rocking slowly in the chair next to his on the porch. Whenever she dared to meet his eyes, she saw something there that stunned her, something that might have been love, something that unmistakably was pure, raw desire.

And yet he hadn't touched her. There'd been no more bone-melting kisses, just spine-tingling, sizzling looks. He was so careful to avoid even the most casual contact that she almost screamed with frustration. Her skin heated with anticipation whenever he neared. Her entire body ached with longing. These old, familiar, unfulfilled yearnings were driving her flat-out crazy.

"You okay?" Jessie asked when Kelly called her on Friday. Five days of skirting Jordan had taken their toll and obviously it showed in her voice.

"No," she said succinctly.

"Uh-oh, what's Jordan done now?"

"Nothing."

"Isn't that what you wanted?" Jessie asked, sounding vaguely confused.

"Yes...no." She sighed heavily. "Dammit, Jessie, I don't know anymore."

Instead of offering the sympathy she'd anticipated, her friend chuckled. "Oh, sweetie, I'm sorry, but watching the pair of you doing this dance of seduction is wearing me out."

"How do you think I feel?" Kelly retorted.

"Let me ask you something. You admitted to me that you love him, so that's not the issue, is it?"

Leave it to Jessie to cut straight to the chase. "No."

"And he obviously cares enough about you to want to spend the rest of his life with you and to raise Dani as his own. He may not call it love, but it's definitely a commitment, right?"

"Yes. What's your point?"

"Don't get mad at me for asking this, but do you think you might be holding out to punish him for all those years when he never gave you a second glance?"

"That's absurd," Kelly said indignantly. "What would be gained by that?"

"Satisfaction, maybe," Jessie offered. "Tormenting him might be a kind of sweet revenge for all those years you spent silently suffering."

"Absolutely not. That's not the kind of person I am."

"Not normally, I know, but these are unusual circumstances. It might be natural to want to exact a little revenge because he flaunted all those other women in your face. I'm not saying that's what's behind your indecision here, I'm just suggesting you think about the possibility.''

Jessie's suggestion angered her. She didn't like thinking she was capable of exacting revenge for deeds she thought she'd long since forgiven, deeds that had never been meant to hurt her in the first place. Still, she knew her friend wouldn't have mentioned it if she didn't think there might be some validity to it.

''I'll think about it,'' Kelly agreed.

In fact, she thought about little else for the rest of the day. She recalled all the instances when Jordan had spent hours on end talking about the hottest girls in high school and asking her advice on how to get them to go out with him. Not that he'd had that much trouble. Even as teenagers, girls had gravitated to him because of his good looks and fun-loving personality. It hadn't hurt that he was a star athlete, too.

He'd been equally sought after during his one year in college, chased when he'd been working the oil fields, and on every year's most eligible bachelor list once he'd settled in Houston. He'd had more relationships than she could count, but when each one had ended for one reason or another, he'd always come back to her to lick his wounds. She'd consoled him, boosted his ego with her nonjudgmental adoration, made him laugh again.

And all the while, her own heart had ached.

When she'd finally tired of the pattern, she had turned to Paul Flint and impulsively married him, determined to put Jordan and her wasted emotions behind her once and for all.

But Jordan had refused to stay out of her life. He had befriended Paul, even though he couldn't stand him. He'd stayed on the fringes of their lives, close enough to pick up the pieces when the marriage had fallen apart. The divorce had taken a long, messy year or more after she'd returned to her family's ranch. Jordan had stuck by her through every terrible minute of it.

She'd experienced a wild moment of hope then, sure that it was finally their turn. Within weeks, however, he had announced his engagement to Rexanne. Though Kelly had known better than to hope for the impossible, she had been devastated just the same. She'd shored up her defenses so securely after that that the marines couldn't have penetrated.

All that night she lay awake considering Jessie's question. Was it possible that she was cutting off her nose to spite her face, just to get even with Jordan for not turning to her sooner? Was she holding out for moonbeams, when what he was offering was much more solid?

From practically the first moment she'd ever set eyes on Jordan she had known in her heart that he was the man she would one day marry. That sense of inevitability had taken a very long time to shake. Now, when she'd least expected it, her chance was finally here and she couldn't seem to bring herself to say yes. Was that nothing more than pure perversity?

As Jessie had pointed out, he might not have said the words she desperately wanted to hear. He might not have said he loved her, but he was willing to stand up in front of God and everyone and declare his intentions to love, honor and cherish her for the rest of their days.

In that moment, she made up her mind. If Dani had no objections, if Jordan's determination hadn't wavered, she would say yes.

And then she would dedicate the rest of her days to making sure that neither of them ever regretted the choice they had made.

Chapter Nine

"Mommy, is Jordan going to be my new daddy?" Dani asked the following morning while shoving her French toast around in a puddle of syrup.

The unexpected question brought up the subject that had kept Kelly awake all night long.

"If he has his way, he is," Kelly muttered before she could catch herself.

She hadn't anticipated getting into this before she'd even had her first cup of coffee. In fact, she hadn't intended to get into it with her daughter at all, at least not until the matter was more settled with Jordan himself.

"When?"

"That's hard to say, sweetie. There are some things we have to work out."

"Like what?"

Kelly thought of all the doubts that had chased through her mind. None of them were things she could share with her daughter. "Just things," she said evasively.

Dani studied her intently and apparently concluded Kelly still wasn't convinced that Jordan would make a proper daddy. "I like Jordan," she informed her mother firmly. "I think he would make a very good daddy."

Kelly wondered if her daughter had insights into Jordan that hadn't come to her yet. "Why is that?" she asked.

"He brings me candy."

Kelly refrained from labeling the candy what it was—bribery. Hadn't he tried the very same tactic on her? She'd already told Jordan half a dozen times to cut it out or he'd be paying Dani's dental bills.

"Don't you like Jordan?" Dani inquired worriedly. "You used to be bestest friends, that's what you said."

"Most of the time I like him very much," Kelly conceded.

"More than Daddy?"

Ah, now there was a mine field if ever Kelly had seen one. She had prepared an answer to that long ago, knowing sooner or later that rather plaintive question or one very similar was going to come up. Dani was too precocious not to ask difficult questions about the man who had sired her but spent very little time in her life.

"Your father is a fine man," she said, almost by rote. "He and I just weren't well suited. We were very young and we made a mistake getting married."

Dani contemplated that for a while, then turned a troubled look on Kelly. "Was I a mistake, too?"

Tears sprang to Kelly's eyes. She wrapped Dani in a hug and squeezed, peppering her worried little face with kisses. "Never, not in a million years. You are the very best part of my life. I wanted you more than anything."

"Daddy, too? Did he want me more than anything?"

Kelly cursed the man she'd once been married to for putting her on more tricky turf. Paul had never been inclined to have children, had agreed to Kelly getting pregnant only after frequent arguments. It had been yet another mistake on Kelly's part. She had thought Paul would love being a father, once he'd gotten over being terrified by the idea of it. She'd been convinced he would take to it. He hadn't. It was one reason she'd watched Jordan's behavior with Dani so closely, one reason she had fretted over how well the two of them would get along. Now, thankfully, she knew there was no comparison.

All of which didn't give her an easy answer to Dani's question.

"Your father loves you very much," she said, forcing a note of conviction into her voice that Paul didn't deserve. She wouldn't be the one to ruin his relationship with his child. He was doing that very nicely all on his own. She hoped someday he would wake up and realize how much he'd missed and suffer regrets for the rest of his life.

"Then why doesn't he ever come to see me?" Dani asked.

"Because he's very busy." The excuse came automatically. She'd been uttering it since the day of the divorce. And for a long time before that, for that matter.

"Jordan's busy, too," Dani stated. "He has a great big company to run and he comes. He's been here a whole week now. He even reads me a bedtime story every single night. Daddy never does."

Kelly thought of her ex-husband's difficult childhood, a childhood he'd used to excuse his need for excess, for more money and more women, just to prove his own worth.

"I don't think anyone ever read to your father when he was little," she said, trying to give Paul the benefit of the doubt one more time. "He doesn't realize how important it is."

Dani shot her a confiding look. "Jordan says he likes to read to me."

Kelly had noticed that herself. After his initial reservations, Jordan had seemed to enjoy the quiet evening time with Dani as much as she always had. "Does he now? Did he say why?"

"Because he likes all those stories, but grown-ups look silly reading fairy tales to themselves. He says he's going to teach me to read one all by myself for the times when he's not here." She turned her dark, velvet blue eyes on Kelly. "I really, really hope you make Jordan my new daddy fast."

In an unfortunate bit of timing, Kelly heard the screen door open just then.

"I really, really hope so, too," Jordan chimed in, winking at Dani, who bolted from the table and threw herself into his arms. They both regarded Kelly hopefully.

Kelly might have been able to hold out against Jordan's powers of persuasion for a little longer, just to assure herself that the decision she'd reached in the dark of night made sense in daylight. Teamed up with her daughter, though, he was an irresistible force. She could do a lot worse than Jordan Adams. In fact, she already had.

She lifted her gaze and met his eyes and saw something there that stunned her—uncertainty. Jordan was vulnerable where she was concerned. It was hardly a declaration of undying love, but it was a start, something to build on.

"Set the date," she said.

He didn't bat an eye. "Next weekend," he said, his serious gaze never wavering from hers. "We'll fly to Vegas."

What an appalling idea! Kelly regarded him indignantly. "Not on your life. This may not be a traditional marriage, but we are going to have a traditional ceremony. We'll have the service and the reception right here."

Jordan turned and cast a dubious look around the house, which for all of her hard work was undeniably shabby in spots. "Here?" he protested mildly. "I can't see the governor . . ."

"The governor can come here or he's not invited," she said flatly. "This is our wedding, not a business dinner. We don't have to impress anybody." She shot him a challenging look. "Do we?"

A grin spread across his face. "Not a soul, sweet pea."

Filled with the first faint stirrings of hope at the quick capitulation, Kelly crossed the kitchen and patted his cheek. "This could work out yet, *sweet pea.*"

Jordan glanced at Dani. "Munchkin, wouldn't you like to go out and check on the kittens?"

"But I haven't even finished my French toast," Dani protested. "'Sides, I want to talk about the wedding, too. Can I be a flower girl? My friend Megan was one. She told me all about it."

Kelly didn't think talking was what Jordan had on his mind. Frankly, at this precise moment, it was the last thing on hers, as well. She needed to feel his arms around her, needed to fit her body against his. She wanted desperately to feel all the passion that marriage was supposed to promise, to be reassured that she wasn't making a terrible mistake.

"Sweetie, of course you can be a flower girl," she promised her daughter. "Remember, though, that today's the day we promised to take a kitten over to Jordan's daddy. You have to decide which one."

"And Cody? Don't forget he wanted two."

Jordan winced. "We'll have to talk about that. Cody's gone away for a while. We'll have to find another home for the two he'd picked out."

Dani's face fell. Her lower lip quivered. "But what if we can't?"

"We will," Jordan promised. "If we don't, they can live with us."

Kelly stared at him. "But you said . . ."

He shrugged. "I can't let you go drowning them in the creek, can I?"

"I would never drown them in the creek," she said, shocked by the very idea of such a thing. "Where on earth would you get such a notion?"

He glanced at Dani, who had hung her head. Kelly had never seen a clearer portrait of guilt.

"Danielle Flint, is that what you've been telling everyone?" Kelly demanded. "No wonder everyone's been so eager to claim these kittens."

Dani's expression of guilt quickly fled. Her chin tilted defiantly. "I had to do something. Besides, they're really, really cute. I knew everyone would like them once they got to know them."

Kelly looked up from her daughter's belligerent face to find Jordan's lips twitching with amusement. "Are you sure you're up to a lifetime of this?" she asked him.

"Oh, I think I'll manage," he said confidently. "You've never scared me."

"More's the pity," she said with feeling. "But I was thinking of Dani."

"She's just the icing on the cake," he assured her.

Dani looked from one to the other, clearly puzzled. "What cake?"

"Never mind, munchkin. Go check on those kittens," Jordan said. "Your mom and I have wedding plans to make."

Dani finally climbed out of her chair and ran from the house. The minute she was out of sight, Jordan cupped Kelly's face in his hands. He studied her intently.

"Are you sure?"

"I have been since I was eight," she admitted, suddenly breathless. "You're the one who took a very long time to come around."

He didn't even begin to deny the accusation. "I guess I had to mine through a lot of fool's gold before I could tell I had the real thing right here."

She held the words to her heart. It was as close to an *I love you* as he'd come. "How are your parents going to react?"

"Oh, I suspect Daddy's been figuring on this for weeks now, maybe even years. If he's content with the decision, Mother will be, too."

Kelly sighed with regret. "I wish my parents had lived long enough for this. They always adored you. As hard as they tried, they never warmed up to Paul."

Jordan tilted her head up. "And you? How did you feel about me?"

"Jordan, I said I'd marry you. Don't get greedy."

"Suddenly I want it all," he whispered softly, just before he slanted his mouth across hers.

Kelly was swept away by the kiss, swept away to a time and place where dreams became real and magic filled every hour of the day. It was a place she'd never thought to reach, because she'd always known only one man could take her there.

And now, out of the blue, it was real and every bit as incredible as she'd always imagined.

The wedding plans were completely out of control. Kelly latched onto Jordan's arm when he walked through the door the following Wednesday and dragged him into the kitchen.

"This has to stop," she insisted.

He regarded her warily. "What?"

"Your mother has taken over. A decorator steamrolled through here this morning as if she were preparing for the Normandy invasion." She glared at her fiancé of less than a week. "I will not have it, Jordan. I won't!"

"What exactly was she here to do?"

"She is designing the wedding," she said, a note of disgust in her voice. "Between now and Saturday, she intends to transform this house into a summer garden. She wants to put trellises with roses in the middle of my living room."

He seemed almost as bemused by the concept as she was. "And you don't want them there?"

"I want my living room to look like a living room, not a damned fake garden!"

The expletive apparently convinced him she was at the end of her patience. Jordan reached out and snagged her hand. Somehow she wound up in his lap, with his arms reassuringly settled around her waist and his lips on hers.

"Kissing won't make it better, Jordan!" she warned at one point.

"Are you sure about that?" he inquired, brushing his lips back and forth against hers until her blood sizzled. It did pretty much wipe thoughts of anything else out of her mind.

"It could be helping just a little," she admitted as his lips found a sensitive spot on her neck. A shudder washed through her. "Okay, more than a little."

"Are you distracted yet?"

"From what?" she murmured, giving herself up to the sensations spinning through her.

A knock on the screen door interrupted. Kelly's sigh only deepened when she spotted Mary Adams, her soon-to-be mother-in-law, on her doorstep. She was wearing her going-into-battle shopping outfit of linen pants, a silk blouse and sufficient gold jewelry to impress the most difficult salesclerk. As stifling hot as it was, she looked cool and unrumpled.

"Enough of that, you two," Mary said briskly as she entered without waiting for permission. "It's ridiculous enough that you've only given a week's notice for this wedding, we can't go wasting time on nonsense."

Kelly gazed helplessly into Jordan's eyes and mouthed, Do something!

Jordan stood. He towered over his petite mother, but his size clearly didn't intimidate her.

"Out of my way," she commanded. "I need to see the kitchen."

"Why?" Kelly inquired suspiciously.

"To let the caterer know what's possible and what isn't."

"I was thinking we'd have those little cocktail wieners and maybe some potato chips," Jordan said. "Maybe a big old platter of barbecued ribs."

His mother simply scowled at his teasing as she breezed past. Kelly trailed along in her wake, tugging Jordan with her. Why hadn't they eloped to Vegas as Jordan originally suggested? It would have been better than this armed invasion of strangers that Jordan's mother had planned.

Mary Adams glanced at Kelly. "What about your dress? Perhaps we should have Harlan's pilot fly us over to Dallas this afternoon. I'm sure we could find something on short notice at Neiman-Marcus."

The suggestion explained Mary's attire. Kelly balked at going anywhere to buy anything. "I have a dress," she said adamantly.

Mary looked aghast. "You're planning to pluck something out of your closet? This is your wedding, for heaven's sake, and Jordan does have a certain status to maintain. What you wear will reflect on him."

The comment grated. "Jordan," Kelly said sweetly, "could I see you in the living room?"

She noticed when she finally had him alone that his eyes were sparkling with pure mischief.

"A problem, sweet pea?"

"If your mother does not back off, I swear to you that I'm going to wear jeans for this wedding and serve lemonade and store-bought cookies."

Jordan pulled her against him. "Sounds perfect to me."

She studied him intently, not sure whether she could trust the dead-serious note in his voice. "You wouldn't mind?"

"Actually, I'd rather like to see the governor's face as he sips lemonade and munches a handful of Oreo cookies. He'd probably prefer it over the rubber chicken and hard little peas he usually gets."

Kelly sighed. "He might be perfectly content, but your mother's likely to flip out."

"Sweetheart, it's our wedding. The details are entirely up to you. Just tell me what time you want me here and I'll show up. I could care less about the rest."

"Are you sure?"

"Absolutely."

"Any idea how many people your mother has invited?"

"Nope," he admitted.

"Maybe I'd better ask that before I get too independent here," she said, calmer now that she knew Jordan was in her corner no matter what she decided.

She went back to the kitchen where she found her future mother-in-law tsk-tsking at the size of the stove and refrigerator.

"Kelly, I think it's time for new appliances, don't you?"

"Absolutely," she agreed without hesitation. Her parents had bought the current ones years ago and they were clearly on their last legs. "But I thought fixing the roof and painting were more important."

The concept of budgetary constraint was clearly beyond Mary's comprehension. "Yes, but this is something you can't put off. I can't possibly have the caterer do anything the least bit elaborate without a decent stove or refrigerator." She jotted a note to herself. "I'll take care of it this afternoon. Do you want white again?"

Kelly moved in front of her. "No new stove and no new refrigerator," she said quietly, even though her stomach was churning and her blood was heating to a boil. "This is a wedding, not a home show."

"But what about hot hors d'oeuvres? And your freezer won't even hold a spare pint of ice cream, much less the ice sculpture I've ordered."

"It's ninety degrees outside. Why would you order an ice sculpture in the first place?"

Mary Adams stopped in her tracks and stared. "You intend for everyone to eat outside? My dear, people will be perspiring," she declared as if that were the worse tragedy that could possibly befall anyone. "You simply cannot ask them to deal with all the dust, to say nothing of this sweltering hot weather. Their clothes will be ruined."

"How many people have you invited?" Kelly countered.

Mary avoided looking her in the eye. "Just a few. You did say you wanted it kept small."

"How many?"

"A hundred, more or less."

Kelly gulped. It was even worse than she'd suspected. "That's what you consider small?"

Mary seemed oblivious to Kelly's distress. "Of course, given Jordan's status, there are business considerations, as well as old friends and family," she informed her future daughter-in-law. "I cut it as best I could."

Kelly had guessed the number would be half that high, which was precisely why she'd considered the possibility of an outdoor celebration. This clinched it.

"I see," she said, rather proud of how calm she managed to sound. "And where do you expect these hundred people to fit inside the house? If you think it would be stifling outside, imagine them all crammed in here without air-conditioning."

"Without air-conditioning?" Mary sank down onto a kitchen chair. "Oh, my, I suppose that is a problem, isn't it?" She fanned herself with her little leather notebook. "Darling! Jordan, come in here at once!"

Jordan, who'd apparently taken refuge in the living room rather than get caught between his mother and his bride, came into the kitchen. He glanced warily from his mother to Kelly and back again. "What now?"

"I really think there is only one thing to be done," his mother said briskly, clearly recovered from her momentary shock. "We will have to move the wedding to White Pines."

"Absolutely not!" Kelly insisted, just as Jordan hurriedly said after one glance at her face, "Now, Mother, let's not be hasty."

Mary scowled at the pair of them. "Well, I simply don't know what else to do," she said in that haughty tone Kelly knew she could come to hate. She gestured around her. "This house is simply not big enough or equipped for a wedding. White Pines has all of the latest, industrial-size appliances and the staff is used to dealing with caterers and a large number of guests. This is the most important day of your life, after all. It should be something to remember."

"It's the most important day of *our* lives," Kelly said, her voice tight.

Jordan clearly heard the stress in her tone, because he hurried his mother out of the kitchen. "Mother, let me discuss this with Kelly and we'll get back to you."

Kelly could hear his mother protesting even as she was hustled away.

"Jordan, the wedding is in three days," Mary complained. "You can't possibly wait another moment before deciding."

"We're waiting, Mother. I'll be in touch."

Kelly thought the screen door slammed rather emphatically behind her. She was resting her head on top of her folded arms when Jordan returned to the kitchen and pressed a kiss to the back of her neck.

"Don't get fainthearted now," he murmured.

She looked up at him and tried to blink back tears. The most incredible day of her life was going to turn into a nightmare. It was on a fast track to calamity and she could see no way to stop it.

"Jordan, I do not want to get married at White Pines," she said emphatically. "I do not want to wear a dress your mother has picked out. I do not want a swarm of caterers and strangers around us."

He sat down opposite her and took her hand in his. "What do you want? Just tell me and I'll take care of it."

Something in his voice told her she could trust him to do exactly that. "I want a small wedding. Just family. I want to wear my mother's wedding gown."

At his startled look, she added, "I didn't wear it when I married Paul. I saved it all these years so I could wear it if you and I ever got married." She sniffed and wiped at the tears tracking down her cheeks.

"Consider it done," he promised.

"Just like that?"

"Just like that."

Suddenly she was uncertain. "Is that selfish? Is your mother right about this being important to you for business reasons?"

He laughed. "Sweetheart, my mother thinks every occasion is an opportunity to solidify business relationships. Don't give that a second thought."

"But she's already invited the governor."

"And I'm equally certain the governor has enough events to attend that he won't mind if I call up and tell him we've decided to elope."

"Elope? I didn't say..."

"In a manner of speaking," he added hastily. "I think perhaps we should plan the ceremony for Friday, tell the family they're simply coming here for a rehearsal dinner and let 'em know after it's over that it was the real thing."

Kelly chuckled as she considered how that news would go over with Mary Adams. "Your mother will kill us."

"The most important thing is you and me getting married, right?"

No doubt about that, Kelly thought. She'd been waiting a lifetime for it to happen. "Right."

He stood and dropped a kiss on her forehead. "Then leave the rest to me. Six o'clock, Friday evening, you and I are getting married."

Kelly flew off of her chair and wrapped her arms around him. "Jordan, I do love you."

As soon as the impulsive words were out of her mouth, she regretted them. She hadn't intended to let him see so soon that her heart was on the line. It would have been far better to let him go on thinking that he was making a business acquisition of sorts.

He folded her into his arms and rested his chin on her head. She thought his heart was beating a little faster than usual, thought she detected a faint shudder sweeping through his body. Small signs, but they gave her hope. In time, surely Jordan would be able to say those words. In time...

Chapter Ten

The wedding was going to be as unconventional as the reasons behind it. An hour before the scheduled ceremony Jordan glanced around Kelly's living room and surveyed the hastily accomplished preparations with a sense of amazement. Admittedly he was no judge of such things, but it looked perfect. Informal, romantic and unique, just like the woman he was marrying.

Dear heaven, he was getting married tonight! He had actually won the battle to claim Kelly's heart. He was marrying a woman who'd been a part of his life for so long that he couldn't remember a time when she hadn't been important to him.

His proposal might have been impulsive, but he sensed without a doubt that he'd made the right decision. He and Kelly were a good match. Marriage wasn't nearly so intimidating or confusing when it was approached in a logical manner. Obviously she'd seen that, as well.

"Nervous?" Luke asked, amusement in his dark eyes as he watched Jordan pace amid the bouquets of wildflowers set on every available surface.

"About marrying Kelly? Not in the least," he said candidly. "About Mother's reaction when she finds out this is the real thing, you bet. She's going to pitch a fit. But if this will make Kelly happy, it will all be worth it. Frankly, I'm glad to be getting it over with. I keep thinking Kelly's going to change her mind."

Luke patted him consolingly on the shoulder. "Don't worry about Kelly. She's been in love with you ever since I can remember. As for Mother, she won't stay mad, not for long, anyway. Daddy will be so pleased by all of this, he'll see to it she handles this with her usual aplomb. And as long as he's happy, she won't bat an eye."

Jordan had his doubts, not about his father's powers of persuasion, but about his mother's flexibility. "I hope you're right. I don't want her and Kelly getting off on the wrong foot."

"Standing up to her is the only way to get off on the right foot," Luke said. "Jessie figured that out early on, while she was still married to Erik. She really had to take a stand once the baby was born or Mother would have taken over Angela's upbringing. Mother finds Jessie a challenge, but she doesn't dislike her. Besides, have you had any indication after all these years that Mother has anything at all against Kelly? It's not as if you're marrying some stranger."

Jordan wondered about that. Kelly had seemed more perplexing to him lately than she had in all the previous years he'd known her. "If you say so," he said, glancing anxiously toward the stairs. "I wish they'd hurry up."

"You don't want them down here before Mother and Daddy arrive, do you? Once Mother sees Kelly in her wedding dress and you in your tuxedo, she's going to know something's up. In fact, it might be a good idea for you to hide out in the kitchen for a while with Consuela," he suggested, referring to his housekeeper.

Consuela had been more mother than hired help to Jordan and all of his brothers. When Luke had elected to build his own ranch, rather than remaining at White Pines, Consuela had gone with him after assuring herself that she was leaving Harlan and Mary in the capable hands of her cousin Maritza. She had always loved Kelly, who'd been in and out of the Adams kitchen as a child. The minute she'd heard about the change in wedding plans, she'd insisted on coming along not just as a beloved guest, but to fix the wedding dinner and bake the cake. Unfortunately, she'd lost patience with his hovering hours ago.

"She's already thrown me out of the kitchen once," Jordan admitted. "She said I was in her way." He sighed and looked at his older brother. "I wish we could have talked Cody into coming back for this."

"I know," Luke said. "I tried. I think Daddy did, too. Cody is still hurt and angry and his pride's at stake. To top it off, he's the most stubborn of all of us and he's dead set against ever setting foot in Texas again as long as Melissa Horton is here. At least we can be grateful he found another job in ranching. He's not just bumming around, hell-raising and licking his wounds.''

Jordan didn't find much comfort in that. ''But Wyoming is a long way from home,'' he noted.

''He'll be back one of these days,'' Luke said with the certainty of an older brother who'd had time to observe the behavior patterns of his siblings. ''Cody is as tied to this family as any of the rest of us, maybe even more so. He's the one who took the most interest in our ancestors, the one who cared the most about being an exalted Adams. He got Mother's powerful sense of family and Daddy's mule-headedness. Sooner or later his anger at Melissa will fade and he'll recognize that this is where he really belongs.''

Jordan wished he were as sure. He'd seen Cody the night he'd discovered Melissa with his best friend. Luke hadn't. ''I hope so. I think Daddy's missing him a lot. As much as Daddy grumbled about being displaced on his own ranch, I think he was really looking forward to having more time to travel with Mother.''

''Maybe, but he's too damned young to retire,'' Luke commented. ''He hasn't taken a real vacation in all these years because his heart's been in running White Pines. How much traveling do you think he really would have done before he'd gone nuts?''

''One trip,'' Jordan agreed with a chuckle. ''Maybe two, especially when he figured out how much money Mother could spend in Paris in a week. His willingness to indulge her might have suffered a major setback after that."

They were interrupted by the sound of a car driving up the lane. Jordan peered anxiously through the screen door.

"Mother and Daddy?" Luke asked.

"The minister, thank goodness. At least we'll all be in our places when they show up. Maybe we can even get through the 'I do's' before they guess what's going on."

"Optimist," Luke taunted. His expression suddenly sobered. "I'm happy for you, little brother. Kelly's one in a million, after Jessie, of course. And I can vouch for the joy of starting off with a ready-made family. It's not nearly as intimidating as I imagined."

"I'm relieved to hear it," Jordan said, hugging his brother. "Thanks for helping me pull this off. No one could have ever had a better best man."

"I'm just glad you finally woke up and asked the woman. Jessie was driving me nuts to give you a push, but we both knew you'd just rebel. You've already wasted too many years chasing after the Rexannes of the world."

"Mother liked her," Jordan acknowledged as he went to open the door for Reverend Garrison, who'd been officiating at family ceremonies as far back as Jordan could remember.

"That should have been your first warning," Luke shot back dryly. He grinned at the minister. "How are you, Reverend?"

"Delighted to see another one of you lads tying the knot," he said, shaking Jordan's hand. "Explain to me again about this being a surprise service. Have to say I've never performed a wedding quite like that before. Who's not in on the secret? Surely not the bride."

"Oh, no," Jordan reassured him. "She's most definitely in on it. It's Mother and Daddy. Things were getting a little out of hand with the planning, so Kelly and I decided to do this our own way. As fast as Mother invited people, we turned around and uninvited them. We promised them a huge reception at White Pines in a few months, assuming Mother's started speaking to us again by then. At least she'll be able to plan that exactly the way she wants to."

The minister chuckled. "Seeing how your daddy likes to think he's the one running things in the family, I can't wait to see Harlan's and Mary's expressions when they find out."

Luke and Jordan exchanged a look of complete understanding. "Us, either," Jordan admitted with more than a little trepidation.

He peered out the door again and spotted dust flying at the far end of the lane. "Guess we'll know soon enough how it's going to go over. Luke, you want to warn the bride and get Consuela in here? I don't want to waste a second."

It already seemed as if he'd wasted far too much of his life.

As Kelly gazed at herself in the mirror, Jessie stood back and admired the creamy lace and silk wedding dress that had been Kelly's mother's. "You look beautiful," she told her. "You'll knock Jordan's socks off."

Dani peeked around from behind her mother and stared at her reflection in the mirror. Her eyes widened. "Mommy, you look like a princess, just like the one in my book."

The compliments were exactly what Kelly needed. They calmed the butterflies in her stomach.

"I feel like a princess," she admitted, her cheeks flushed. She had never felt this way before, not even on the day she had married Paul.

She'd had half a dozen attendants then and a church filled with friends and family. They'd even had a string quartet playing as the guests arrived. It had been a fantasy, storybook wedding, but she'd participated without this nervous sense of anticipation, without so much as a flutter of pure excitement. Now, just thinking of Jordan waiting downstairs, her pulse hammered.

"All set?" Jessie asked. "I saw Harlan and Mary drive up a second ago. Luke will be putting 'The Wedding March' on the stereo any minute now."

Kelly reached over and clasped her friend's hand. "Thank you for being here for me."

Jessie smiled. "Where else would I be? I've been waiting for this day for a long time, too. You two were made for each other. Jordan's softer around you, less driven. Given a little time, I think it's entirely possible the man will get his priorities in order."

Kelly wasn't quite so convinced the leopard could change his spots. "I hope you're right. I really don't want to spend any more time in Houston than I absolutely have to."

"Then you'll just have to convince him that modern communications are such that he can run his business perfectly well from right here in west Texas. Give him a modem as a wedding present."

"An interesting idea," Kelly said slowly, giving it serious thought. "There really isn't any reason he couldn't operate the company from here, is there? I'm sure all those vice presidents and administrators he has running around over there would be glad to be out from under his thumb. Maybe I'll have a little chat with Ginger one of these days. She could probably tell me how tricky the logistics would be."

"She's his right arm, isn't she?" Jessie asked. "If you could win her over, it seems to me that would be half the battle."

"I've spoken to her several times when I called Jordan at the office. Her husband is from this part of the state," Kelly said, beginning to see how it could all work out. "From what I gather he's been bugging her to live over this way during the off-season. Says he wants to get back into ranching before he retires from football. She's held out because she loves her job. She doesn't want to be stranded way out here with nothing to do."

"There, you see," Jessie said triumphantly. "All it'll take is a little ingenuity."

"And perhaps a little of Harlan's skill at manipulation," Kelly admitted. "Think he'd give me lessons?"

"I doubt anything would thrill him more. It killed him to see Jordan move that far away. Nothing makes Harlan happier than being surrounded by family."

Before they could get any more carried away with their plans, Dani piped up, "I hear the music, Mommy. I hear it!" She started spinning around. Flower petals scattered from her basket as she twirled.

Jessie picked up Angela, who'd been sleeping peacefully during the preparations. She gazed at Kelly. "Ready?"

Kelly drew in a deep breath, then nodded. "Ready."

Jessie bent down to Dani. "You know what you're supposed to do, right?"

Dani's expression turned serious. "I go down the steps and sprinkle rose petals all the way to the living room until I get to Jordan."

"Exactly right," Jessie confirmed, and opened the bedroom door. "Let's have a wedding!"

Kelly watched as her daughter descended the stairs, then began her slow walk into the living room, self-consciously scattering the flower petals. When Luke winked at Dani as she passed, Kelly could see the familiar, impudent grin spreading across her child's face.

Then, from the living room, she heard Harlan's exclamation of pride and Mary's enthusiastic praise of their soon-to-be granddaughter.

"Oh, how darling!" Mary Adams exclaimed. "Dani, you look absolutely precious."

Kelly didn't hear what was said after that, because suddenly Jessie was moving down the steps in her pale blue dress and her own grasp on the banister tightened into a death grip. This was it. After all these years of waiting and hoping, after all the disappointments, her wedding to Jordan was finally only a few minutes away. She had more than enough trepidations, but as many as there were, they were no match for the joy that was radiating through her. She was sure her smile was as big as Texas as she began the walk to Jordan's side.

She took each step slowly, savoring the anticipation of the instant when Jordan would see her, praying that he would be pleased, praying even harder that the cool deliberation behind his proposal would be transformed into pure emotion on this day. When he vowed to love her, she desperately wanted to see in his eyes that he meant it.

Then, practically before she knew it, her hand was in Luke's and he was walking her into the living room. With no one to officially give her away, he was serving double duty as best man and her escort. He patted her hand reassuringly and leaned down.

"You'll make him happy," he whispered with conviction. "Never doubt that." He winked then. "And if he doesn't do the same for you, let me know and I'll beat him up for you."

Impulsively Kelly stopped where she was and stood on tiptoe to kiss the cheek of this man who'd been her champion since childhood. "I'm so glad I'm going to be part of your family."

"It should have happened long ago," he said, his expression suddenly serious. "But you know how stubborn we Adams men are. One thing about us, though, once we make up our minds, we're steady as the Rock of Gibraltar.''

"I'm counting on that." She drew in a deep breath, then made the turn into the living room.

She was dimly aware of Mary's soft gasp of astonishment, vaguely aware of Harlan's whispered exchange with his wife. It was one thing for Dani and Jessie to be dressed up for the rehearsal, another entirely to see the bride in her wedding gown. Superstition alone would have precluded it.

"What on earth?" Mary exclaimed, gazing from Kelly to her husband and back again.

Kelly was oblivious to whatever Harlan said in response. Her gaze was locked with Jordan's. His eyes shone when he saw her. She suspected his throat had gone dry, because he swallowed hard.

And then he smiled. Heavenly days, what that smile did to her. Her stomach flipped over, her pulse skipped crazily. Suddenly, as Luke placed her hand securely in Jordan's, her heart was filled to overflowing.

"Dearly Beloved..." the reverend began.

The rest was a blur. Kelly knew she made the appropriate responses because no one had to prompt her. Still, the only thing that seemed at all real was Jordan's firm grip on her hand and then the cool slide of gold as he slipped the wedding ring on her finger. She noticed, too, that his hand trembled ever so slightly when she slid a thicker, matching band of gold over his knuckle to rest in the place where it would remain for the rest of their days.

"I now pronounce you husband and wife," the reverend intoned. "You may kiss the bride."

Jordan's warm lips grazed hers, lingered, then claimed her mouth more hungrily. Kelly's knees went weak. She looked up and met Jordan's intent gaze. Rock-solid, dependable Jordan. Her husband! Just looking into his eyes steadied her. There was no uncertainty in his expression, no hint of doubt in the depths of his eyes.

They had done it, she realized as Jessie kissed her cheek and Luke pumped his brother's hand. They had actually gotten married just the way she'd envisioned, surrounded by those dearest to them and no one else.

Dani held up her arms to Jordan, who promptly lifted her up. "You're my daddy now, right?" she demanded, clearly dismissing the man who was biologically responsible for her birth but had done nothing to earn a secure place in her heart.

"I am your daddy," he concurred, an unmistakable note of wonder in his voice. Pride shone in his eyes.

Well satisfied with the incredible bond that had formed between Dani and Jordan, Kelly dared a glance at her new mother-in-law. Confusion was written all over her face. Kelly left Jordan's side and went to speak to her. She took Mary's cool hands in her own.

"Please, don't be too angry with us."

"You're married?" Mary said, sounding faintly bemused, rather than furious. "You're actually married?"

"We really are. We both wanted a quiet, intimate celebration. We talked about eloping, but we very much wanted all of you here. I hope you're not too disappointed."

Mary shook her head, as if trying to shake off her confusion. "But all of the guests, the arrangements..." Her voice trailed off helplessly.

Still holding Dani, Jordan came over and dropped a kiss on his mother's cheek. "All taken care of," he assured her. "I spoke with everyone and told them they'd receive an invitation to a reception at White Pines later." He regarded her intently. "If you're still willing to plan a party for us."

Mary stood there, her expression uncertain, until Harlan moved in.

"Of course, we will. We'd be proud to, wouldn't we, Mary?" He tugged Kelly into a tight embrace. "Welcome to the family, girl. It took too damned long to make you one of us. I for one couldn't be more pleased."

He glanced over at Dani, who was still clinging to Jordan's neck as if she was afraid to let loose of this new, attentive daddy she'd just acquired. "As for you, young lady, I think you've got all the makings of a real Adams," Harlan declared. "You bargain with the best of them. Next thing you know you'll be running that oil company of Jordan's. As for that kitten you talked me into taking, she's already queen of the barn."

"Want another one?" Dani inquired. "I think maybe Francie is going to have kittens again."

Jordan shot a horrified look at her that had his father and Kelly laughing. "Oh, no," he muttered. "I'm having both of those cats fixed first thing tomorrow."

The old tomcat, who'd slipped out of the kitchen to wind between Jordan's legs, meowed a violent protest at the threat.

"What a disgusting conversation for your wedding day," Mary chided, clearly recovered from her initial shock. "Jordan, I do wish you'd remember the manners you were taught."

He leaned over and kissed her again. "Are we forgiven for not telling you about the wedding ahead of time?"

Kelly watched her mother-in-law closely, saw the momentary indecision, then caught Harlan's quick squeeze of her hand. Mary rallied at once, her impeccable breeding and her adoration and respect for her husband overcoming whatever disappointment she was feeling.

"Of course you're forgiven, darling. A surprise wedding will have everyone talking. People will be absolutely desperate to receive invitations to the party your father and I will throw for you."

As Jordan and Luke had predicted, their mother was clearly in her element. She would be able to plan exactly the sort of celebration she wanted. All Jordan and Kelly would have to do was show up. It seemed like a suitable arrangement to Kelly. She surely would have bungled something crucial and Mary would never have forgiven her. Now the burden of pulling off the reception would be totally on Mary's capable shoulders.

"Come, come," Consuela called from the doorway to the dining room. "The wedding dinner is ready."

As the others went off to sit down, Jordan held Kelly back. She shot a questioning look at him. "Everything okay?"

"I just had the most incredible need to kiss my bride."

She tilted her chin and met his gaze. Those butterflies in her stomach took to doing somersaults. "Any particular reason?"

"Because you're beautiful and because that official kiss at the end of the ceremony was over far too quickly to suit me," he murmured as he settled his mouth firmly against hers.

As always, it was the touch of velvet and fire, inflaming her even as she tried to think about the guests who were waiting for them a few feet away. "Jordan," she whispered dazedly.

"Mmm?"

"Your family."

"They're our family," he corrected. "And they can wait. We're newlyweds, remember? We're expected to spend a lot of time kissing."

His lips claimed hers again. His tongue invaded her mouth, teasing, inviting, sending her senses whirling. Finally, when she could barely stand, he ended the kiss, though he continued to hold her pressed tightly against his body. His heat surrounded her, drew her in. His masculine scent, counterpointed by the aroma of the flowers that filled the room, made her heady with longing.

"I had no idea," he murmured.

"No idea about what?"

"That I could ever want anyone this desperately."

He sounded shaken by the sudden discovery, shaken and more than a little pleased, she observed.

He was no less pleased than she. She'd spent years all too familiar with the desperate yearning that had just struck Jordan for the first time. And, she realized with both astonishment and anticipation, in a matter of hours a lifetime of longing would finally be fulfilled.

Chapter Eleven

It was amazing how quickly Jordan managed to rush everyone through a four-course meal and a wedding cake. Kelly almost felt sorry for their guests, who were hustled out of the house with all the finesse usually reserved for door-to-door salesmen.

As bad as she felt, though, she did absolutely nothing to delay their departure. Ever since that kiss had practically knocked her stockings and her traditional wedding garter off, she'd been counting the minutes until she could finally be alone with the man she had loved for so many years. They'd planned a few days here all alone as their honeymoon.

To her chagrin, she'd barely spared a glance for her daughter, who'd gone off eagerly with Luke and Jessie, excited about her first opportunity to help babysit her new cousin Angela. She knew Dani would be in good hands with Jessie and Consuela there to look out for her. For the first time since Dani's birth, she was able to be purely selfish for just a little while. She intended to cherish these few days of quiet, private time with Jordan right here in the home she intended to share with him for the rest of their days.

As the last car drove off, she was finally left alone with her brand-new husband. Suddenly she felt absurdly shy. She glanced at Jordan as if he were a blind date she'd never seen before. Given the haste with which their status had changed from friends to mates, she realized belatedly that she hadn't yet fully made the mental adjustment to their new, untested relationship.

Marrying a best friend shouldn't have been nearly so scary, she thought, battling unexpected panic. Perhaps if they'd had a normal courtship, perhaps if they'd been intimate or at least shared more than a few deep, steamy kisses, she wouldn't have felt like blushing every time she looked at him. Somehow, though, going from best friend to lover in a heartbeat filled her with uncertainty. She felt as if her entire world had shifted crazily and she'd been left off-balance.

All of the insecurities that had welled up in her when she'd discovered her ex-husband had been turning to other women returned now with doubled intensity. Failing Paul had been one thing. Failing this man she loved so deeply was something else entirely. She wasn't sure she'd be able to bear it if she disappointed Jordan.

As if he sensed her turmoil, Jordan took her hand in his. "We're going to be okay," he reassured her.

Kelly lifted her gaze to his. "It's just that this feels so strange," she confided.

"Scared?"

"A little."

"Why?"

Since he seemed honestly interested in the answer, she began to relax just a little. She kicked off her shoes, settled herself on the sofa and accepted the glass of wine he held out. Seated beside her, he waited patiently as she struggled to find an explanation that would make sense to him.

"I think what scares me the most is the possibility that we'll mess up what we already have," she began cautiously. "You're the very best friend I've ever had. You've always been there for me. You can practically read my mind. It seems like we're putting that at risk for something that's far less certain."

His lips twitched. Amusement danced in his eyes. "Do you mean sex, by any chance?"

Kelly swallowed hard and nodded. "It changes things, complicates them."

"Or enhances them," he suggested quietly. "Sweet pea, we can take this slow, if that's what you want. I know I pushed hard for you to make this decision. I hardly gave you any time at all to think, probably because I was afraid you'd say no if you really thought it over. If you're not ready to make love, we'll settle into being married awhile first."

His understanding made her want to weep. He was being so damned nice, so *reasonable*. Perversely, she wanted to smack him. Why wasn't he sweeping her off her feet, using his considerable experience to seduce her?

"Don't you want..." she began uncertainly, all of her fears crashing down on her and filling her with dread.

Shock spread across his face as he apparently realized what she was most afraid of. He reached for her then and pulled her into his arms. The gesture alone began to dispel her doubts, but it wasn't enough. She waited, breath caught in her throat, to hear what he had to say.

"Of course, I want to make love," he reassured her. "I've been wanting to for weeks now. Do you know how many times I've left here aching for you?" He took her hand and pressed it lightly against his arousal. "See, that's what being close to you does to me. I seem to have developed this craving for touching you."

Stunned by the discovery that Jordan really did want her, Kelly's irrational fears fled as rapidly as they'd escalated. Panic gave way to frantic desire. She twisted to face him and cupped his face in her hands. Her thumbs skimmed over the faint stubble on his cheeks, relishing the rough texture that she'd yearned for so long to feel.

"It will be okay, won't it?" she asked, a note of pleading in her voice.

"More than okay," he promised. "This marriage of ours is going to last forever and it's going to be filled with passion and laughter. I'm going to make you happy, Kelly."

She smiled at the determination she heard in his voice. "You already have," she whispered against his lips. "You already have."

With Kelly snuggled next to him on the sofa, still wearing the wedding dress that had once been her mother's, Jordan felt more serene, more complete than he had in months, maybe even years.

He understood the doubts and uncertainties that had assailed her after everyone had left. Her lousy marriage had robbed her of the confidence she'd once had in spades. He intended to give it back to her.

Admittedly, though, he'd had his own moment of panic earlier, when he'd seen her coming down the stairs in a swirl of silk and lace. The tomboy he'd grown up with, the best friend he'd always relied on had been transformed into a fairy-tale princess, just as Dani had confided to him seconds before her mother had appeared.

The hope and trust he'd seen shining in Kelly's eyes at that moment had frightened him. What if he couldn't be the husband she deserved? What if his impulsive decision to claim her for himself short-changed her? He'd been thinking mostly of himself when he'd proposed marriage. He'd tired of the chase, of the unceasing test of wills with women he never seemed to understand. He'd been anxious to settle down. Most of all, he'd wanted to do that with someone he knew and understood, someone uncomplicated.

From that instant on, however, he'd discovered that Kelly was perhaps the most complicated of any of the women he'd ever known and his feelings for her were far more complex than he'd ever imagined. When she'd appeared before him in her wedding gown, a vision of unexpectedly fragile loveliness, he'd wondered for the space of a heartbeat what he'd gotten himself into, if he was up to the challenge of making her happy.

And then she had been beside him, her hand tucked trustingly in his and he had known not another second's doubt. He smiled to himself, satisfied that the gut instinct that often led him to take quick, decisive action in business had served him well in choosing a mate.

She stirred slightly in his arms, drawing his attention to the way her breasts shifted against his chest. Her wedding dress was hiked well up her shapely calves.

He thought again of her misplaced doubts and smiled to himself. Oh, he wanted her all right! For days now he'd been able to think of little else but making her his. He'd wanted to caress and explore and inflame. He'd wanted her to come apart beneath him and he wanted to see the flare of excitement and satisfaction in her eyes. He wanted to discover all of the facets to this woman, who'd suddenly become so incredibly intriguing to him, so sweetly, unexpectedly desirable.

"Jordan?"

"Hmm?"

"This is nice."

"What is?"

"Sitting like this, with your arms around me."

Nice? It was killing him. "Aren't you hot with that dress on?" He'd stripped off his tuxedo jacket and tie long ago, but the room still felt stifling to him. To be honest, though, maybe the heat was emanating from him. Each time Kelly squirmed even a little, his body temperature rose another degree. Given the flush in her cheeks, she had to be feeling the same sort of heat, as well.

"I am hot," she confirmed. "But I'm too comfortable to move."

"What if I were to carry you upstairs?" he suggested in a choked voice.

"An interesting idea," she replied, a teasing glint in her eyes.

"Was that a yes or a no?"

"I think a yes," she said, then hesitated, before bestowing a tremulous smile on him. "Definitely a yes."

Jordan's heart was suddenly beating so hard he wasn't sure he'd heard her correctly. "Now?"

"Now."

With an eagerness that was far too telling, he scooped her into his arms. Cuddled against his chest, she looped her arms around his neck and settled her head against his shoulder. Her sweet breath fanned against his cheek. He was so stunned by the sensations spinning through him, he almost dropped her. A primitive need combined with an instinctive protectiveness swelled inside him.

Tightening his hold on her, he carried her up the stairs and headed straight for her bedroom. In the doorway, he came to a shocked and dismayed halt.

The room was in chaos, filled with the scattered, feminine debris of two women and one child getting ready for a wedding.

"Whoops!" she murmured, then chuckled at the sight. "I'm sorry, Jordan. Put me down. I'll have it all cleaned up in no time."

"Isn't there a guest room?" he asked, not even trying to hide his sense of urgency.

She grinned. "Sure there is. You know this house as well as I do, Jordan."

"Well, then?"

"Twin beds," she reminded him.

He groaned. "We'll manage."

"Jordan, you're over six feet tall and I'm not exactly petite. If you think I'm sleeping in a twin bed with you, you're nuts."

"Who's talking about sleeping?"

"Okay, doing anything with you in a twin bed. One of us is bound to topple to the floor."

At the image she'd created, he felt a chuckle begin deep in his throat. "Exactly how energetic, are you?"

She blushed to the roots of her hair. "Jordan!"

"Okay, okay, I'll help you straighten up in here." He reluctantly lowered her to her feet. Before she could even move, he was tossing things off the bed and onto the floor. To his sincere regret, she was trailing along behind him, picking up each item and folding it neatly before tucking it away in a drawer or closet or laundry basket.

"Do you have to do that now?" he demanded impatiently.

"Jordan, you have waited years to get me into bed. In fact, for years, you didn't appear the slightest bit interested in getting me to bed. Can't you wait a few more minutes so it will be perfect?"

He found the equation between tidiness and perfection a bit disconcerting. "As long as you don't decide to start ironing, too, I suppose I can wait." He caught her gaze and held it. "And just so you know, I did think about getting you in bed back then. I just figured your father or mine would aim a shotgun straight at my backside if I did. I thought I was displaying admirable restraint in treating you like a lady."

She grinned at him, obviously pleased by the discovery that she had the upper hand over him in this. In fact, she looked downright smug all of a sudden.

"Go downstairs and find some candles," she ordered every bit as imperiously as her daughter might have.

"It's still daylight."

"Twilight," she corrected. "It'll be dark soon and I want candles."

He sighed. "Anything else?"

"Bring back the wine, too."

"Got it," he said, heading out the door.

"And some flowers," she called after him. "Lots and lots of flowers."

He poked his head back into the room. "You're enjoying this, aren't you?"

"What?" she inquired with a look somewhere between pure innocence and very feminine satisfaction.

"Tormenting me."

"Is that what I'm doing?"

"Yes, dammit," he shot back, but there was little venom in his voice.

He actually found her playfulness another delicious surprise. The delay was tantalizing. As if he didn't already want her badly enough, his body was practically throbbing with need now. There was no way she could possibly have any doubts at all, after this, about how hungry he was for her. Torment was a small price to pay for reassuring her on that point.

To even the score just a little, though, he took his own sweet time to gather up the candles, flowers and wine she'd requested. Let her stew a little, too, he thought as he finally made his way back upstairs. If the sexual tension mounted another notch or two, they would probably burst into flames on contact.

Back upstairs, at the doorway to the room, he came to a screeching halt for the second time that evening, stunned by the sight in front of him.

She had used the time very efficiently. Not only was the mess cleared away, but she had somehow managed to shed her wedding gown and exchange it for a filmy white negligee that skimmed over her curves, revealing details about her body he'd only imagined before. Her back was to him, the fading light from outside just enough to enhance the intriguing vision before him.

"Dear heaven," he murmured, stunned into immobility. His throat went dry.

Turning to look at him over her shoulder, she gave him the kind of soft, knowing smile women had been bestowing on infatuated men for eons. It sent a shudder of pure desire sweeping through him.

"I thought you were beautiful before, but I was wrong," he said in a strangled voice. "You are magnificent."

Surprisingly, the comment drew a look of uncertainty. "You don't have to say that."

"I do," he insisted, hastily setting flowers, wine and candles on the nightstand beside the bed and reaching for her. "You are magnificent."

She came into his arms without hesitation, fitting her body to his with an eagerness that turned his breathing ragged. Her anxious fingers worked at the studs on his shirt. As it came open, she pressed hot, quick kisses against his bared chest. The touch of velvet soft lips and warm breath sent his pulse spinning wildly.

"Whoa," he murmured. "Slow down, sweetheart. We have all night."

He glanced into her eyes then and read more than desire there. He detected once again that uncertainty and realized that until he claimed her in a rush of uncensored passion, she would be filled with doubts. About him. About whatever seeds of uncertainty Paul had planted in her brain with his shabby treatment of her.

There would be time enough later for long, slow, deliberately sensual seduction, for discovery. There were years ahead of them for lazy caresses and deep, passionate kisses. Thousands of nights lay before them, nights of sultry breezes and whispered exchanges as they learned intimate secrets about each other's body.

When her trembling fingers reached for the button on his pants, he helped her, shucking them off along with his briefs, after kicking aside his shoes.

Pulling her tightly against his hard, anxious body, he tumbled carefully onto the bed with her. He rolled her on top of him as they fell, exulting in the natural fit of soft curves and hard angles.

He never took his eyes from hers, not when his hands skimmed over her full, sensitive breasts, not when her hands reached for his aroused manhood. He saw the moment when her eyes darkened with passion, saw the instant of surprise when he fit his body to hers, entering her with a hard, fast stroke that had her gasping and her hips lifting to meet each thrust.

And he witnessed in the depths of her eyes the precise second when her body shattered in a climax that rocked them both. The satisfaction that streaked through him then, the wonder of giving her pleasure, was like a miracle. He'd had no idea that making love could be like this.

She was still panting, still exhilarated when he took her on another, slower climb that had her eyes widening with astonishment and then pure delight as they reached the pinnacle together and dove off into yet another whirlwind of sensation more magnificent than anything Jordan had ever experienced before.

He wasn't sure which was more heady, watching Kelly reach the heights of joy or sharing it with her. Together, they brought him immense gratification.

Eventually, exhausted and satiated, he settled Kelly more tightly against his body, his arms around her waist, her head resting on his chest.

She was certainly full of surprises, this woman he'd married. Once again, he indulged in a moment of smug satisfaction with his decision making. Obviously it was possible to use cool logic when choosing a bride. The passion they'd just shared reinforced his confidence.

Kelly propped herself up on her elbow and stared down at him. Her fingers tangled in the hair on his chest, then skimmed over bare, still damp skin.

"What are you thinking?" she asked.

"About us," he replied without hesitation.

She appeared instantly fascinated. "What about us?"

"How well suited we are. In bed and out. It just goes to prove my point."

A shadow crossed her eyes. "What point would that be?"

"That people should use their brains more often when choosing a mate."

"As opposed to what?"

He heard the edginess in her tone too late. By the time he met her gaze, her eyes were frosty, the brown glinting with angry amber lights. He tried to back off the quicksand he'd inadvertently wandered onto. "Never mind," he muttered and tried to distract her with a caress.

She brushed away his hand and sat up, clutching the sheet to her. "I think you'd better tell me, Jordan."

He saw that he was way too far into this now to escape. "Come on, Kelly, you know what I mean. We both used our heads in deciding to get married. We didn't have a lot of silly illusions. We made a sensible decision that will benefit both of us."

"In other words, a successful merger." Her voice was heavily laced with chilly disdain. She gestured at the rumpled bed. "And this? I suppose this is just one of the perks for the executives?"

Actually, it was, but he was wise enough to keep that particular observation to himself. "Now, Kelly..."

She climbed out of the bed, dragging the sheet with her. He was certain no one had ever exited a marriage bed with more dignity, with more icy contempt.

"Don't you 'now, Kelly' me," she said, waggling a finger under his nose. "I made love to you tonight, Jordan Adams. I did not seal a damned business deal!"

With that she stalked from the room, the sheet trailing after her like the train of an impromptu bridal gown. Unfortunately, Jordan had the distinct impression that not only the honeymoon, but quite possibly the marriage, as well, was over.

Chapter Twelve

Kelly was still steaming at dawn when she heard Jordan coming slowly down the stairs, his steps heavy. She'd been on the front porch most of the night, wrapped in her sheet, rocking in an attempt to calm her fury.

It hadn't worked. Now, anticipating him joining her on the porch made her blood boil and her palms sweat. She'd wanted another hour or two to get her temper under control and all of her defenses solidly into place. When she faced him again, she had hoped to be cool, calm and collected. She was nowhere near that when he appeared.

Dressed in a pair of faded jeans, unsnapped at the waist, his hair becomingly tousled, his eyes still sleepy, Jordan opened the screen door and stepped outside. Looking at him made her heart climb into her throat.

She refused, however, to let the mere sight of him get to her. Loving him so desperately, wanting him, was what had made her suspend judgment and agree to marry him when she'd known better.

Discovering that he still thought of their marriage as some sort of twisted business arrangement within seconds of also discovering that their passion was extraordinary had left her reeling. It confirmed every dire prediction she had made for a future built on such flimsy turf.

Even though he was waiting, she refused to meet his gaze.

"Good morning," he said eventually, sounding wary.

She remained stubbornly silent.

"Still mad, huh?"

Huddled in the rocker, she refused to utter a word.

Jordan was not a man easily defeated. He walked in front of her so she couldn't ignore him and hunkered down. He put his hands on her thighs to still the rocker. The touch guaranteed her attention.

"I'm sorry," he said. "I swear that I didn't mean to upset you."

She scowled at him. "But you did mean what you said, right?"

He stood and raked his hand through his hair in an impatient gesture. "Yes, no, ... Hell, what do you want me to say? Do you want me to lie to you?"

A good white lie might be welcome about now, she thought irrationally, then sighed. "No, I suppose not."

"Sweet pea, we just need a little time to adjust. This is new to both of us. Once we're settled in Houston..."

Warning bells went off in Kelly's head. " 'Settled in Houston'?" she repeated very slowly. Her gaze locked with his. "I am not settling in Houston. We agreed to split our time. Weekends, holidays and vacations here. Weekdays there. That was the deal."

She made sure there was no mistaking where she put the emphasis. She managed to make the time they would spend in Houston sound like exile in Siberia. Jordan blinked at her adamant tone.

"We did discuss that, but—"

"No buts," she insisted, cutting off any speculation that there was room for more negotiation. "We agreed."

"Let's be reasonable," he began again.

She wasn't in the mood to be reasonable. Being reasonable and practical and pragmatic—to say nothing of caving in to her hormones—was what had gotten them into this disastrous situation.

"We had a verbal contract," she said, throwing his favorite sort of terminology back into his face. "Are you trying to wriggle out of it?"

He winced, but didn't back down, either. "Now, Kelly..." he began in a placating tone that set her teeth on edge.

"Forget it. We can end this marriage just as quickly as we arranged it," she warned.

Even as she spoke, she spotted the stubborn thrust of his chin and recognized that she might have pushed Jordan too far. She didn't much care. If this marriage wasn't going to be a partnership, if his promise of compromise had been so much hot air, they might as well discover it now.

"We are not ending this marriage," Jordan said quietly, eyes blazing. "As for where we live, we'll work it out."

"We already have," she said again.

His jaw tightened. "Fine. Pack your bags. We'll pick up Dani first thing tomorrow and drive back to Houston."

Kelly was shaking her head before the words were out of his mouth. "Not tomorrow. I can't leave the ranch with no one in charge."

"No problem. I'll call Daddy. He can deal with your hand to make sure chores get done until we make other arrangements."

"But the cats . . ."

"The damned cats will be taken care of. Weekdays in Houston," he reminded her, throwing her own words back in her face. "We'll settle anything having to do with the ranch next weekend. Daddy can screen some candidates for foreman while we're gone."

Backed into a corner now, he wasn't going to budge on this. If she intended to hold him to the letter of their verbal agreement, then he clearly planned to hold her to it, as well. Kelly could see that from the fire in his eyes and the clenching of his jaw. The gene for stubbornness, carried by both Harlan and Mary Adams, had clearly doubled in Jordan. Kelly tugged the sheet more tightly around her and rose as regally as any queen.

"Why wait? I'll be packed in an hour."

He scowled. "Fine, if that's what you prefer. I'll make some coffee and some breakfast. As soon as we've eaten, we can drive to Luke and Jessie's."

Kelly could only begin to imagine what those two would have to say about Kelly and Jordan appearing on their doorstep first thing in the morning after their wedding night. The prospect was damned humiliating, but she refused to back down and ask Jordan to at least delay their departure until Sunday after all.

Let him explain why their honeymoon had ended so abruptly. He thought he had all the answers. Let him see how well they held up to his brother's scrutiny. Maybe she'd even take Luke up on his offer to punch his brother out for her. No doubt he hadn't imagined there would be a necessity for it quite this soon.

Still seething, she threw clothes into suitcases with almost as little care as she'd displayed when leaving Houston after her divorce. She gathered up a few of Dani's favorite toys and resolved that her daughter would be allowed to pick out a new selection for the Houston house. If they were going to be shuttling back and forth, then each home needed to have its own set of clothes, toys and books. She refused to pack and repack every few days. The same went for everything from cosmetics to toothbrushes. Two complete households, she decided firmly. Let Jordan put that in his pipe and smoke it.

And, first thing on Monday morning, she intended to have a very long talk with Ginger about the logistics of moving Jordan's primary business offices home to west Texas.

In fact, she might very well take the secretary to lunch and probe her brain for the secrets of tolerating her husband's high-handedness. She had always considered herself to be an expert on Jordan, but she'd seen a new side of him in the past few weeks—a man all too used to getting his own way—and she had a feeling Ginger knew far more about that side than she did.

Refusing to ask for assistance, she hauled the luggage downstairs and piled it by the front door. Lured by the aroma of coffee, she reluctantly headed for the kitchen and another confrontation with her husband.

Jordan glanced up from the morning paper at her entrance. "I have pancakes and bacon staying warm in the oven. Sit down. I'll get it and pour you a cup of coffee."

"Just coffee and juice for me, and I'll get it."

He scowled at her as he stood. "Sit, dammit. I said I'd get it."

Kelly rolled her eyes at the testiness and sat. He poured the coffee, filled a glass with juice and then reached into the oven to retrieve the breakfast he'd prepared. Suddenly he yelped in pain and jerked his hand back. His bare hand.

Kelly sighed and stood. Jordan obviously wasn't thinking any more clearly this morning than she was.

"Let me see," she said, reaching for his hand.

"It's fine," he growled.

"Let me see," she said, and clamped her hand around his wrist. There was a nasty streak of red across his palm that was destined to blister. She tugged him toward the sink. "Here, run cool water on it and I'll get some salve."

He stood stoically while the water cascaded over his burned hand. She retrieved the ointment she kept on hand for burns. Taking his hand in hers again, trying not to notice the way her pulse jumped at the contact, she gently applied the soothing salve, then wrapped the wound lightly in gauze.

She was so intent on bandaging his hand that she didn't notice the intensity of his gaze for some time. When she finally glanced up, the fire banked in his eyes was every bit as hot as the plate he'd tried to pick up.

She released his hand at once and turned her back on him, busying herself with getting the offending plate from the oven, turning off the stove and then sitting down at the table to eat the breakfast she'd claimed not to want. It might as well have been sawdust for all the attention she paid it as she swallowed bite after bite mechanically.

"We can't avoid talking about it forever," he observed eventually.

He'd tilted his chair back on two legs and clasped his hands on top of his flat stomach in a posture that screamed of relaxed confidence. She risked a look directly into his eyes. "Talking about what?"

"The fact that we've gotten off to a lousy start."

She shrugged. "We both know it. Why talk about it?"

A look of annoyance passed across his face. "So that we can resolve the problem and move on."

Kelly's temper flared. "How...businesslike!"

He stood up so fast, then, that his chair toppled over. Before she realized what he intended, he was leaning over her, bending down, his mouth unexpectedly plundering hers in a bruising kiss clearly meant to wipe all other thoughts out of her head. After a brief struggle of wills, it succeeded in doing just that. Her mind emptied of everything except the way Jordan made her senses swim. She abandoned the battle and gave herself up to that devastating kiss.

His lips gentled, then, coaxing, persuading, reminding her of the way they'd been together in the middle of the night—hot, slick sensuality, mind-altering pleasure, gentle sharing. They were good together, as instinctively attuned as two people who'd been married for decades. Jordan was the kind of sensitive, intuitive, giving lover women dreamed of finding. He had gauged her reactions time and again and suited his lovemaking to her needs. He was doing the same thing now.

Eventually he released his grip on her shoulders and stood back, his gaze fixed on her in a way that told her he was taking in her flushed cheeks and the kiss-swollen lips that clearly told him the effect he had on her. For once, though, he seemed more dazed than smug.

Observing him, Kelly thought how ironic it was that they were so instantly attuned physically, while all the years of straight talk had abandoned them and left them suddenly incapable of communicating in words without bickering.

She gathered her composure and drew herself up. "I think it's time to go," she said in a voice that shook.

For a moment she thought he might argue for staying right here, for settling their differences in bed, but he didn't. After a bit, he just nodded curtly.

"I'll get the bags into the car," he said.

"I'll clean up in here and be right with you."

It was all so cool, so polite and civilized that she wanted to scream. Instead, the instant he was gone and she was left alone with soggy pancakes and cold coffee, she felt tears welling up in her eyes.

She'd had the wedding of her dreams the day before. She was married to the man she'd always loved. She'd discovered a passionate side to herself and to him that had filled her with ecstasy.

And she'd never been more miserable in her entire life.

Jordan would rather have faced a firing squad than Luke and Jessie's worried, accusing looks. Their gazes darted between him and Kelly, their eyes filled with questions that only Dani's presence had kept silent since their arrival.

"So, you're driving back to Houston?" Jessie said with obviously feigned cheer, her gaze penetrating. "Do you have to be back in the office first thing Monday? You are supposed to be on your honeymoon, after all. Surely the incomparable Ginger could hold down the fort a few days longer."

Jordan glanced at his wife. Kelly's cheeks were flushed with embarrassment. She'd looked everywhere but at him since they'd arrived. He couldn't decide whether he wanted to console her or to shake her.

Dammit all, he hadn't wanted to head back to Houston today any more than she had. He still wasn't quite sure how it had happened, except that she'd dug in her heels and then he'd dug in his and their disagreement had escalated from there. Somehow he'd forgotten how often that used to happen to them as kids. They were both quick to anger and stubborn as mules. It had always taken Luke or Cody to coax them out of their funks.

He glanced at his older brother and caught a grin tugging at Luke's mouth. Obviously he was recalling the same thing. The amused reaction left Jordan feeling faintly disgruntled. Clearly he couldn't count on much help from that direction. Luke seemed perfectly content to let him and Kelly work this fight out all on their own.

"I'm sure Jordan and Kelly have their reasons for going to Houston today," Luke observed, confirming Jordan's opinion of his brother's intention to stay the hell out of this argument.

Jessie didn't appear to have the same reticence. "What reasons?" she demanded, frowning. "Dani's perfectly fine here with us, aren't you, sweetie?"

Dani nodded. "I'm helping Consuela take care of Angela. She's messy."

The comment drew a faint smile from Jordan. "I can vouch for that," he murmured.

"Hey, that's my daughter you're maligning," Jessie said. "Dani, honey, why don't you go check on her? She's with Consuela."

As soon as the child had run off to the kitchen, she turned her determined gaze back on Jordan. "Okay, explain."

Jordan swallowed hard under the scrutiny. "I don't think so."

Jessie looked from him to Kelly. "Kelly?"

"Ask Jordan."

Luke laughed out loud at that. "Maybe their reasons are none of our business," Luke suggested.

Jessie did not seem pleased by her husband's observation. "Of course, it's our business. We're talking about your brother and my friend."

"That doesn't give us inalienable rights to interfere," Luke shot back.

Suddenly, to Jordan's astonishment, Kelly chuckled. "Stop it, you two. The next thing we know, you'll be fighting and you won't even know why."

Jessie regarded her intently. "Do you know why you're fighting?"

Kelly considered the question thoughtfully. "I know," she said. "I'm not so sure Jordan does."

He frowned at that. "Hey, don't make me into the bad guy here."

Luke gazed heavenward. "How many times have I heard those words from you two? You'd think after all these years, you'd learn to fight fair."

"I'm not the one . . ." Kelly began.

"Whose side are you on, big brother?" Jordan demanded.

"Ah, the sweet sound of two stubborn personalities butting heads yet again," Luke said. "Jessie, maybe we should back off and let them fight it out."

"Not in my living room," she countered. "I do have a compromise, though."

At the mention of compromise, Kelly's gaze caught his. He wasn't sure but he thought he detected amusement dancing in her eyes. "Bad idea," he told Jessie. "I'm afraid compromise is what got us into this argument."

Jessie wasn't about to be put off so easily. "That's not possible. Compromise is good."

"Not necessarily," Kelly muttered.

"Well, you'll just have to listen to mine," Jessie declared. "If you two absolutely must go to Houston, wait and leave in the morning, let Dani stay here until you come back. At least you'll have some privacy for the next week or so. It may not be a honeymoon in the Caribbean, but it's the best I can offer on short notice."

Jordan glanced hopefully at Kelly. Given time, he knew they could work this disagreement out. It would go much more smoothly if they didn't have Dani to worry about. It was Kelly's call, though. He wasn't about to start their marriage by forcing her to leave her daughter behind. He didn't ever want her to think that he wasn't interested in all of them being a family. Unfortunately, she didn't look overjoyed by the suggestion.

"I don't know..." She looked at him, clearly struggling with the prospect of abandoning her child even for a few days. "Jordan?"

"It's up to you."

"Come on," Jessie urged. "It's the perfect solution. She's having a wonderful time here and she's no trouble at all. You were planning for her to be here a few days anyway. Besides, you don't want her caught up in the middle of your argument, do you?"

Jordan watched Kelly debating with herself, clearly aware of the sense of Jessie's suggestion, but resisting it just the same. He kept silent and let her work it out on her own.

"I suppose it would be okay just this once," Kelly agreed eventually. She shot a determined look at Jordan and added, as if daring him to contradict her, "We'll pick her up Friday evening."

"Absolutely," he agreed.

Still looking worried, she gazed at Jessie. "Are you sure it won't be an imposition?"

"Absolutely not," Jessie said. "Right, Luke?"

Luke cast a quick look Jordan's way. Jordan gave his older brother an almost imperceptible nod.

"Right," Luke agreed.

"And you'll stay the night," Jessie prodded.

Clearly Kelly would have preferred to eat dirt, but she nodded. Jordan figured he had till morning to think how to mend fences.

They were on their way at daybreak. Dani hadn't batted an eye at their departure, but Kelly had been misty-eyed ever since.

"Are you sure you don't mind leaving Dani here?" Jordan asked after he'd made the turn onto the highway. "There's still time to change your mind."

"No, I think it's best that you and I resolve some things before we try to get on with having any kind of normal family life. Jessie was right. Dani heard enough fighting between Paul and me. I don't want her to go through that again."

Jordan studied her intently. "Are we going to fight?"

She sighed and met his gaze. "It seems inevitable, doesn't it?"

"What seems inevitable to me is being married to you," he said at once. "The rest of it is just details."

Kelly's startled expression gave way to something that might have been relief. "Do you really mean that?" she asked.

"I never say anything I don't mean," he assured her. "Sometimes I don't phrase things tactfully enough. Ginger's always getting on me about that. Sometimes I cut to the chase too soon, but I always, always mean what I say."

He slowed the car and eased it onto the shoulder of the road, so he could look directly into her eyes. "When I stood in front of that minister night before last and promised to love, honor and cherish you all the rest of our days, I meant every word." He leveled a gaze straight at her. "Did you?"

Tears shone in her eyes and her lower lip trembled as she nodded. "I did."

"Then, like I said, sweet pea, all the rest is details."

Chapter Thirteen

The very first detail Kelly intended to deal with was getting the two of them out of Houston permanently. She had forgotten how heavy and oppressive the air there could be in midsummer. Clothes clung damply the minute they stepped out of the car. The movement between stifling heat and air-conditioning was capable of inducing pneumonia, especially since Jordan kept his home at Arctic-level temperatures. A chill sped through her at the blast of cold air that hit her the instant he opened the huge, carved front door.

Other than the frigid temperature, Kelly really had nothing against Jordan's house. She'd been in it dozens of times when she had lived in Houston. She'd always admired the neat sweep of perfectly tended lawn, the cool turquoise waters of the pool, the thick,

lush wall-to-wall carpeting, the decorator-chosen selection of fine paintings and antiques.

None of it, though, seemed to have anything to do
with Jordan, at least not the man she knew. What
frightened her was the possibility that it might reflect
this other Jordan, the shrewd businessman she wasn't
nearly so fond of, the man who bargained for a bride
with the same single-minded determination with
which he'd go after an oil contract.

Only his study, with its book-lined walls, its slightly
faded Southwestern decor, its original Remington
bronze sculpture, seemed to fit his personality or his
taste. The rest was too formal, too sterile.

And she could just imagine how long it would take
Dani to destroy all those yards and yards of white
carpeting that had clearly been chosen by someone
without children or, worse, by someone who never
intended to have children.

Children? Dear heaven, they hadn't even discussed them except in the most passing way. What if
Jordan really didn't want more? What if all that white
carpet had been the idea of a man who saw his house
as a showplace rather than a home? What had happened to her brain? Why hadn't she asked the most
basic question of all? *Do you, Jordan Adams, want
a family?* Paul had certainly taught her that was
something that couldn't be taken for granted.

Seeing Jordan with Dani must have reassured her,
but she'd been a fool not to ask anyway. Making as-
sumptions was the worst sort of mistake a woman
could make, especially when it was a lesson she
should have already learned.

Standing in the doorway, her thoughts in turmoil, she was startled when Jordan lifted her off her feet to carry her across the threshold. She was struck anew by the enormity of what they had done. Somehow, even more than the vows they'd taken, the traditional act of being carried across the threshold into Jordan's home, onto Jordan's turf, reminded her of all the unanswered questions, of the compromise she had agreed to to be with this man she loved. A renewed sense of panic set in.

Apparently oblivious to her shift in mood, Jordan set her carefully back on her feet in the huge foyer, then took her hand as he led the way upstairs for the first time.

It was late. The drive had taken forever and they had stopped often, rarely talking, just grabbing a bite to eat or a tall, cool, soft drink to soothe their parched throats. Going to bed seemed only logical, but Kelly wasn't ready for that. She couldn't seem to form the words, though, that would halt their inevitable progress up that wide, winding staircase. Being alone with Jordan in Luke and Jessie's guest suite sure had been hard enough. This was awful.

At the doorway to the master suite, he paused. "Kelly?"

She heard an unfamiliar note of uncertainty in his voice and met his gaze. "What?"

"I want you to be happy here. I want us to be happy."

He seemed to be imploring her to reassure him that their quick, impulsive marriage was moving onto more solid ground. Unfortunately, she had too many uncertainties herself to be able to say exactly what he clearly wanted to hear.

Instead she gazed across this threshold into a room she hadn't seen before. In all of her previous visits she'd studiously avoided so much as a peek at a room that had seemed emotionally off-limits to her as Jordan's friend, rather than his lover. She hadn't wanted to see the bed to which he took other women but never her.

Now, she surveyed the dark furnishings that had been someone's idea of a bachelor's taste and opted for a touch of humor. "You could go a long way toward making that happen by getting rid of the fur bedspread and the waterbed."

As she'd hoped, he grinned. "The fur's not real."

"No, but without it, you could probably raise the thermostat another ten degrees."

"Too cold in here?"

"Not if you're wrapped in that thing."

He chuckled. "Okay, I get the message. Now, about the waterbed. Have you ever slept in one?"

"No."

"Don't knock it till you've tried it."

"Jordan, I get seasick. You couldn't even take me out on the creek in a rowboat, remember?"

He turned an interesting shade of green at the memory. "I'll have it out of here in the morning," he promised. "Of course, we should check to make absolutely sure it's a problem."

Kelly regarded the bed doubtfully, but there was such a gleam of pure anticipation in Jordan's eyes that she kept her doubts to herself. "If you say so."

She approached the king-size waterbed tentatively. There was something incredibly seductive about it, especially with that expanse of soft, fake fur spread across it. She sat down and tested her stomach as the bed shifted beneath her. The ebb and flow of the water was disconcerting, but not entirely unpleasant.

"Well?" Jordan asked, his expression hopeful.

"So far, so good," she admitted.

"Mind if I join you?"

She eyed the bed nervously. "Not as long as you don't fling yourself on the bed and set off a tidal wave."

Clearly amused, he dropped down beside her. His weight set off another softly rolling wave.

"Ready for the next step?" he inquired.

"Which is?"

"Getting out of our clothes."

She stood hastily and backed off a step. "I think I'll do that on firm ground, thank you very much."

"But you will be back?"

She gazed into worried blue eyes and sensed a deep concern for getting things off to the right start here in his home. "I will be back," she promised, then amended, "Tonight."

"And tomorrow?"

"Maybe we ought to take one night at a time," she said, casting a suspicious look at the bed. "You might not even want me back in there tomorrow if this doesn't go well."

"Maybe not in *this* bed," he agreed with a mischievous smile that reminded her of the Jordan of old. "But, like I told you before, this can be out of here first thing in the morning and one more to your liking in its place."

His expression sobered. "I want you to make this your home, to make whatever changes are necessary to make you and Dani comfortable here."

Kelly kept silent about her intention to see that this was their home for as brief a time as possible. Instead she inquired, "Can I get rid of the white carpet?"

"Every boring inch of it," he agreed readily.

His response, indicating his distaste for it, surprised her. "Exactly whose idea was that?"

He sighed. "Rexanne's."

"I should have known. Obviously she wasn't the maternal type."

"Do you really want to waste time discussing my former fiancée?"

"Did you have something else in mind?" she asked, even though she could see perfectly well by the gleam in his eyes exactly what he was thinking.

"Getting you back into this bed would be a start."

Kelly pushed aside the memory of all of the angry exchanges earlier in the day. She deliberately squashed any thoughts of that terrible moment when she'd realized that Jordan's perception of their marriage hadn't changed drastically from the moment he'd first gotten the idea into his head and pursued her with single-minded determination.

In fact, she suspended thinking at all, clinging only to the promise that they could work out the details and make their marriage a real one.

She stripped quickly out of her clothes and moved into the waiting circle of his arms, into the heat emanating from his body. She lost herself to the gentle movement of the bed and the swell of anticipation in her heart as his hands caressed and stroked until every inch of her was on fire, burning with need.

She welcomed him into her, lifting her hips to meet him, opening her mouth to his tongue, then gasping with the sweet, sweet shock of coming apart in his embrace.

Worries and fears didn't vanish in that moment of surrender, but, for a time, they hardly seemed to matter at all. All that mattered was being close to Jordan, fulfilling the hunger that had been building inside her since she'd first discovered the chemistry that was possible between a man and a woman.

The rest would still be there in the morning. She could tackle the problems then with a clearer head and a lighter heart. Or so she told herself as she drifted off to sleep, still resting her head against Jordan's chest, reassured by the steady rhythm of his heart and the unmistakable strength in the arms that held her tight.

Jordan thought the first night in their Houston home had gone rather well, all things considered. He had no doubt at all that the basic disagreement between them still existed, but when they were in each other's arms, little else seemed to matter.

That was what kept him from rolling out of bed at first light and heading to the office as he routinely would have done. He was reluctant to leave this ha-

ven they seemed to have found away from their differences.

Propped on an elbow beside her, he watched as
Kelly slowly came awake. A soft smile came and went
as she blinked, saw him, then closed her eyes again.
A pleased, sensual expression remained on her face.
He realized it was the first time he'd ever watched her
wake up in the morning. She did it slowly, easing into
the day in a way he found thoroughly fascinating.

"What time is it?" she murmured eventually, eyes
still tightly shut.

"Six-thirty."

"I should be up."

"Why?"

"There's work..." she began, then let the sentence trail off.

"Nope," he reminded her. "You're on vacation."

She sat up, bringing the sheet with her and tucking
it around her breasts. Jordan reached over and tugged
it down. "Don't be shy with me," he said. "Please."

Though color climbed into her cheeks, she left the
sheet where it had fallen, exposing her breasts to the
chill air. The nipples puckered and hardened even as
he watched. He swallowed hard against the tide of
raw desire rolling through him. He couldn't resist,
though, touching a finger to each sensitive peak. He
was thrilled by the shudder that instantly swept
through her.

"You are amazing," he whispered hoarsely. "Your
body is so responsive."

"Jordan, don't you have to go to work?"

He couldn't tell from the ragged note in her voice if she was anxious for him to go or stay. "Sooner or later," he murmured.

"Wasn't that the reason we came to Houston?" she asked.

He was too fascinated with the way the morning sun was casting highlights and shadows on her smooth skin to pay much attention to the note of determination in her voice. "Hmm?"

"I asked if the reason we are in Houston is so that you can go to your office," she said.

This time it would have been impossible to miss the edge of exasperation in her voice. "Actually, we are in Houston because you made an issue of that damned compromise."

As soon as he'd snapped out the retort, he realized his mistake. Up went the sheet . . . and the wall between them. He sighed heavily and climbed out of the suddenly cold bed. This time he didn't intend to stick around to repair the damage.

"If you want me later, I'll be at the office," he said stiffly. He took his clothes into the bathroom. "As you made clear, that is the only reason you agreed to come here." With that, he slammed the door.

It appeared they were destined to have a far more volatile marriage than he'd ever anticipated, at least if he kept opening his mouth. Every time he did, he managed to put his foot squarely in it.

Kelly refused to linger in that huge waterbed all by herself, not with Jordan slamming things around in the bathroom and cursing a blue streak. She seemed to be testing his patience, which was just fine with her. Hers had snapped a long time ago.

Downstairs, she snatched up the phone and dialed his office. As she'd anticipated, Ginger was already at her desk.

"Hey, Kelly," the secretary said at once. "How's it going?"

Kelly wasn't about to give her the earful that question deserved. "Fine."

"If you're looking for Jordan, he's not in yet. In fact, I thought he was still over at your place trying to talk you into marrying him."

"He won that battle," Kelly said dryly. "We're into the full-scale war now."

"Uh-oh," Ginger murmured. "What can I do?"

"Are you free for lunch?"

"Why, sure. I'm getting sick of eating those little cartons of yogurt at my desk. You want to meet me here at noon?"

"I think we'd better meet at the restaurant." She named one close to Jordan's office. It was the same one he had traditionally taken her to when they'd met to catch up on each other's lives in what now seemed a far simpler time in their relationship. "Is that okay?"

"Sure thing. See you there at noon."

"Meanwhile, prepare yourself. My husband is in a snit."

"Well, damn," Ginger said. "I was hoping marriage to you would mellow him out."

"Not so far," Kelly admitted grimly.

She spent the next half hour staying out of Jordan's path. It wasn't all that difficult. He appeared to head straight from the bathroom out the front door without so much as a backward glance. It was an interesting route given that the more logical access to the garage was through the kitchen where she was seated drinking her coffee. She was beginning to wonder if perhaps she shouldn't have had this little meeting with Ginger *before* the wedding.

She sighed. Too late for second thoughts now. She just needed a refresher course in what made her husband tick. All those tips she'd stored away since childhood needed to be updated to deal with the grown-up idiosyncrasies.

A few hours later, after taking a taxi into town, she was seated in a booth across from the perky, sensible redhead who was Jordan's right arm at the office. Ginger was scrutinizing her with obvious fascination.

"Okay," she said finally, "how'd he talk you into it?"

Kelly shrugged. "I wish I knew. One minute I was saying no, no, no, and the next thing I knew I was standing in front of a minister saying I do."

Ginger nodded. "He has that effect on people. I can't tell you the deals that seemed on the verge of falling through, only to turn completely around at the last possible second. You've known him forever, though. You should be immune to his tactics."

"He's never tried these particular tactics on me before." She chuckled. "And frankly, I doubt he's used the same ones in business."

"Ah," Ginger said knowingly. "*Those* tactics."

"Among others. He got Dani on his side, too, and that pretty much sealed the deal."

"How's he taking to being a daddy?"

"Oddly enough, that seems to be the part of all this he has nailed. He's a natural. He and Dani are like co-conspirators, always making plans and whispering secrets."

"Sounds as if you feel left out," Ginger observed.

"Not at all. I'm thrilled they get along so well. I just wish he and I could communicate as easily."

Ginger's face fell. "But you two were always able to talk. I envied you. DeVonne's not big on communication." She grinned. "Not verbal communication, anyway. You and Jordan, though, could always talk about anything. He used to say that all the time."

"I guess that must have been before the stakes got to be so high."

"Meaning that marriage changes things," Ginger concluded. "Maybe that's because it's almost impossible to lose a best friend, but people are getting divorced all the time. You've already been through that, so you know it's a real possibility. That makes you start pulling your punches, being less honest than you ought to be, am I right?"

Kelly gave her a rueful grin. "I'm not sure Jordan would agree that I've been pulling any punches, but actually you're exactly right."

"Seems to me like that's the perfect way to ruin the best thing you two had going for you."

"It is, isn't it?" Kelly murmured thoughtfully. "Ginger, you're a genius."

The young woman grinned back at her. "Well, of course I am." She sighed. "Now if you could just convince Jordan to move our offices to west Texas."

Kelly laughed. "You're reading my mind. That was the other thing I wanted to talk to you about today. Is that feasible?"

"Why, sure it is. He might have to fly here for meetings every so often, but half of what he does can be done by phone and fax. I've been telling him that for ages now, but he's too bullheaded to listen. If you ask me, he was just afraid if he moved back, he'd be under his daddy's thumb again."

"Harlan's not even in the oil business," Kelly protested, though she didn't doubt for a second that Ginger was exactly right.

"You know, I love that man, but Harlan does have his opinions. It doesn't seem to matter that he's not in oil. He still manages to offer Jordan unsolicited advice about a dozen times a week."

"And what does Jordan do?"

"Sometimes he puts him on the speaker phone, mumbles an appropriate response when the occasion arises and gets on with his paperwork. Those are the good times. Then there are the times when he slams the phone down so hard it breaks. I've taken to keeping a new stock of telephones in the supply closet. The phone company loves those calls. It's probably paying Harlan to make them."

Kelly couldn't help chuckling at the image. It was vintage Jordan and Harlan. They'd always scrapped like willful, territorial puppies. She was still laughing when she heard a polite, masculine cough and looked up to find her husband's watchful, suspicious gaze focused straight on her.

"Something amusing?" he inquired.

Kelly swallowed hard. "Actually, yes."

Ginger, the little traitor, bounced out of the booth as if she'd heard a fire alarm. "Thanks for lunch, Kelly. Congratulations, again!"

Kelly nodded distractedly, her gaze locked with her husband's as she tried to gauge his mood. "Thanks for...everything."

Ginger scooted past Jordan. "'Bye, boss."

"Ginger," he acknowledged coolly. He slid into the space his secretary had vacated. "You two catching up?"

"Yes." Suddenly the booth felt very crowded. It wasn't just Jordan's size, but all those suspicions he clearly had.

"Or conspiring?" he asked.

"Now what on earth would we have to conspire about?"

He shrugged. "Beats me. Maybe moving the office to west Texas?"

Kelly groaned. "You heard."

"Every word," he confirmed. "And I do not break phones when I talk to Daddy."

"Oh?"

"I break them after, when I throw them across the room."

She chuckled. "You're not really furious at me for talking to Ginger, are you?"

He sighed. "Why would I be furious? You were asking a question, one that unfortunately plays right into Ginger's hands. She's been bugging me to make the same move for ages, so she can keep her job and her marriage."

Kelly figured he hadn't exploded yet, so she might as well pursue the point. "So why haven't you considered it?"

"It never made sense. My life was here."

"Your business life or just Rexanne and all of her predecessors?"

His mouth twisted into a wry smile. "Probably the latter more than anything."

"But that's no longer true. Now your social life—your family life—is clear across the state." She reached over and put her hand on top of his. "Please, won't you just think about it?"

He studied her intently. "Does it mean that much to you?"

"Yes," she said firmly. "It does."

"Do you hate Houston so much? Is it because of Paul?"

She shook her head, not entirely willing to explain the whole truth of it. Her disastrous marriage was one element, but actually a very small one. Then she recalled what Ginger had said about pulling punches.

"I never wanted to live in Houston," she admitted finally. "I love the ranch, always have."

"But you moved here years ago, right after I did."

"Exactly," she said softly. "Right after you did."

She saw the precise moment when the explanation registered.

"You moved here *because* of me?" he asked, clearly astonished. In fact he couldn't have looked any more shocked if she'd announced she wanted to take up stripping.

"Yep. Pretty crazy, huh? Half the time you didn't even notice I was around." She had abandoned her father to struggle along alone for a man who hadn't even paid attention to her presence. The knowledge of that betrayal of her dad had eaten at her for years.

"But I always thought..." He shook his head, as if to clear it. "I guess I don't know what I thought."

"You just took my presence for granted," she said, unable to hide the note of resentment, even after all this time.

He nodded slowly. "I suppose I did." He lifted his gaze and looked her squarely in the eyes. "I'm sorry. If I'd known—"

She stopped him with a touch of a finger to his lips. "If you'd known, you wouldn't have done anything differently. My heart was always on my sleeve, Jordan. You just didn't want to see it."

He closed his eyes and sighed. "I was a fool, wasn't I?"

She nodded, not letting him off the hook easily. "I always thought so, but then, I was a bit biased in my own favor. Those women you were choosing over me were airheads."

He brought her hand up to his lips and kissed the work-roughened knuckles. "Will it really make you happy for me to move the company headquarters?"

"West Texas is home, Jordan. It's where our family is, where our roots are."

"More's the pity," he said dryly.

She chuckled at his expression. "Stop worrying about Harlan. You've been standing up to him for a long time now and I haven't noticed either of you suffering too much as a result."

"I suppose not," he conceded. "Okay, sweet pea, we'll give it a try. I'll keep the Houston office space for meetings that can't be held elsewhere, but I'll look for space for a new headquarters when we're home this weekend. I'll have to see how the rest of the staff feels about relocating to determine how much space we need, but a lot of the people would probably prefer a small-town atmosphere for raising their families."

Kelly regarded him with astonishment. He'd agreed. Just like that, and all because she'd worked up the courage to tell him straight out what was in her heart. Perhaps if she kept it up, they could work out the rest of those complicated details, starting with whether or not Jordan wanted to have more children.

Before she could tackle that subject, though, she met his gaze and caught the rising heat in his eyes. He wanted her, again, after all those times during the night. Her pulse skittered crazily and her self-esteem as a desirable woman soared.

"Do you have to go back to the office?" she asked.

He grinned. "You were reading my mind."

He took care of the check with the speed of a man very anxious to make love to his new bride. He had them in the car and home before Kelly could gather her thoughts.

Much, much later, wrapped in his arms, she teased him about kidnapping her from the restaurant.

"Hey, you were the one who asked if I had to go back to the office," he protested.

"How do you know I wasn't going to suggest a shopping excursion?"

The look he directed at her was almost comical. "You wanted to go shopping?"

"Maybe."

"You did not." He slid his hand between her legs. "Would you rather buy a dress than do this?"

She grinned. "Maybe."

His touch intensified. "Really?" he taunted. "I don't believe you."

"I haven't shopped for a fancy designer dress in quite some time. It would take a lot to compete with trying on all those fancy, sexy clothes," she managed to gasp. His mouth closed over her breast. "Of course, this is nice," she murmured.

"Nice? Nice!" His voice climbed indignantly.

"Very nice."

He lifted himself above her and entered her with exquisite slowness, the slow slide a sweet torment. The retreat left an agony of yearning. "How nice?" he demanded.

"Incredibly, wickedly nice," she declared.

And then, for quite some time, she couldn't speak at all.

Chapter Fourteen

The next few days in Houston turned into a honeymoon, after all. It was a time of revelation for Jordan. His bride turned out to be a woman of limitless and astonishingly inventive passion. She held nothing back.

Except, perhaps, for love, he realized despondently as he sat alone in the dark sipping a cup of coffee just before dawn on Saturday morning. They had driven back to the ranch via Luke and Jessie's the night before, arriving late. Kelly and Dani were both still sleeping upstairs. He'd been too restless to sleep, troubled by something he couldn't quite pin down or put a name to.

The past few days should have left him feeling ecstatic. He should have been filled with contentment, delighted with the way his decision to marry Kelly had turned out. Instead he had the uneasy feeling that he'd lost more than he'd gained.

For a woman who had stunned him with her claim just a few days before that she had loved him forever, Kelly had suddenly turned surprisingly silent on the subject of her own emotions. He certainly couldn't complain about their lovemaking. She was stunningly sensual in bed, as generous with her body as she had once been with her compassion and her affection. He told himself that should be more than enough, that the words didn't matter, but deep inside he recognized something she had known all along—they did matter.

He couldn't help wondering—and worrying just a little—about her reticence. Something crucial seemed to be missing from their relationship. There was some part of her that she wasn't sharing, that she was holding back as if she feared he might trample on something she held dear.

What more could he do, though? He thought he had made it clear to her that he believed in them, believed in their marriage. He had even agreed to look for a new headquarters for his company, one closer to home, just because she had told him how important that was to her. Surely that gesture should have reassured her that his intentions toward their future were serious.

Dammit, he should have been on top of the world. He had gotten exactly what he wanted. He had a family now, a defensive barrier against another stupid mistake with the wrong woman. He had been granted the unexpected gift of a warm, passionate wife. He even had a precious little girl, whom he couldn't have loved more if she'd been his own.

What was happening to him? Why did it suddenly seem to matter so much whether Kelly cared half as deeply for him as he was beginning to suspect he did for her? They were married, committed to vows they both held sacred. Still, he wanted more, some indefinable thing he didn't know how to describe, much less fight for.

He had seen it, though. He had seen it between his parents, a glow that came over them whenever they were in the same room. He had felt it every time he'd been with Luke, Jessie, and little Angela. He had seen the radiance on Jessie's face whenever she glanced at Luke. He had caught the unmistakable pride and adoration on his brother's face each time Luke glimpsed Jessie or the baby. As with his parents, the air around Luke and Jessie hummed with the electricity of their love. No one lucky enough to be in their presence could ever doubt the depth of their feelings for one another. *That* was what he wanted.

There were times like now when Jordan wondered if he'd truly gotten married or, as Kelly had often accused, merely made a bargain. The irony, of course, was that a few weeks ago he hadn't known the difference, no matter how often Kelly had tried pointing it out to him. Apparently he should have listened to her more closely. Maybe then he would have grasped the distinction, maybe then he wouldn't have set himself up for this unfamiliar emptiness deep inside him.

Now he wondered if it was too late to change the ground rules. He thought of all the unexpected things

Kelly had brought into their marriage, along with being a woman he knew he could trust with his life. He thought of what the future might be like without her in it and realized that losing her was a risk he could never take. Just as Cody had blown it with Melissa Horton, he had taken Kelly for granted. As much as he disliked what that said about him as a man, he knew it was true. He also knew he would never do that again.

Sitting there as the sun rose and brightened the kitchen, he examined the dilemma with the same methodical logic he would apply to a business problem. He considered every angle, weighed every option. When the solution finally came to him, he was astounded he hadn't recognized it sooner.

The answer was a baby, a link that would bind them together more snugly than the vows they'd taken.

A baby! The very thought filled him with unexpected anticipation. The role of daddy had turned out to be one for which he was surprisingly well suited, after all. A little brother for Dani, maybe a little sister, too. The perfect family.

Contentment stole through him as he contemplated the image. Pleased with himself, he charted a course. Now all that remained was to get Kelly thinking along the same lines.

Surely, it would be easy. She adored Dani. From the day of Dani's birth, Kelly had thrived on motherhood. In fact, Paul's disinterest in being a parent had been the primary cause of trouble between them, along with his philandering, of course. Jordan predicted she would be thrilled with his thinking, as ready to embark on this new, shared commitment as he was.

Of course, he warned himself, as he began preparing a breakfast feast to get her in the proper mood, Kelly hadn't exactly been predictable lately.

No matter, he told himself blithely. When he set his mind to something, he could be very persuasive. He'd gotten her to marry him, hadn't he? By comparison, this battle ought to be little more than a skirmish, an easy victory.

"You want to have a baby?" Kelly asked.

She knew she was staring at Jordan as if he'd announced a desire to bring an elephant into their lives, but she couldn't help it. If he had made such an announcement, suggesting the adoption of a huge gray beast, she couldn't have been any more astounded.

She abandoned the special waffles he'd prepared, obviously to set the tone for this conversation, and pushed aside her plate. She laid her fork carefully back on the table, buying time, hoping to figure out what the devil was going on with her husband this morning.

"Why?" she demanded eventually. The question wasn't all that complex, but it certainly cut to the heart of the matter.

Jordan seemed dumbfounded that she'd asked. She could see by the darkening of his eyes that it wasn't the reaction he'd been hoping for. At this precise moment, however, she was more interested in a little honesty and straight talk than she was in catering to some whim of his. The man hadn't once mentioned children except in the most passing way. In fact, she had worried about his silence on that very topic. Now he expected to snap his fingers and produce a child in nine months.

Rather than being eager to agree, she found herself filled with caution.

"Why?" she repeated more emphatically, since he seemed to be ignoring the original question.

Patches of color darkened his cheeks. "Isn't that what couples do?" he said defensively. "You always said you wanted a houseful of kids. Have you changed your mind?"

The last of her foolish eagerness fled at his tone. Kelly shook her head. "No. I love children," she said dully.

"Well, then, that settles it."

The man clearly didn't have a clue about the fine art of holding a conversation, much less a discussion. He was much better at issuing edicts. "Do you really think it's that simple?" she asked.

"I think it can be, if we're both agreed."

Exasperated, she waved aside the too quick answer. "Are we both agreed? What do you want?"

"A baby," he repeated, clearly bemused by what he apparently considered her pigheadedness.

"Why?" she persisted, trying one more time to get to the real reason for this sudden interest in procreation.

Heaven knew, she would give anything to have Jordan's baby, but not without exploring the subject in a little more depth. She'd been too eager once before and discovered too late that Paul had gone along with her only to get her off his back. That might not be the case with Jordan, but perhaps he was only anticipating her desires and trying to settle the matter before it became an issue between them. After all, he'd witnessed firsthand the way the same topic had affected her marriage to Paul.

In so doing, though, he was the one to make it an issue. She studied him intently and waited for his answer.

"The usual reasons," he grumbled.

"And what would those be?" she inquired stubbornly, drawing a ferocious scowl.

"Dammit, do you or do you not want to have a baby?" he snapped.

I want you to love me, she cried to herself. *I want a baby that is a product of our love.* "I do," she said finally, "but not until we're sure we're ready."

"I'm sure."

"You keep saying that, but you haven't said why."

"Isn't that obvious?"

"Not to me."

He glowered at her irritably and stood. "I'm going for a walk."

Kelly nodded curtly. "You do that. And while you're gone, perhaps you'll come up with an explanation for this sudden decision of yours."

Judging from the way he slammed the door behind him on his way out, she had a feeling he was going to be too busy cooling off to think clearly about much of anything.

Blast it all, when was he going to learn that he couldn't just make unilateral decisions for the two of them and expect her to fall into line? He'd done it when he'd decided on marriage. She was determined he wouldn't get away with it when it came to electing to have a baby. They would not bring a child into this world until Jordan could say without reservations that he loved her.

She sighed at that and resigned herself to a long wait. He was as clueless now about what would really make her happy as he had been weeks ago.

"Mommy, where's Jordan?" Dani asked sleepily as she wandered into the kitchen, once again wearing her favorite Dallas Cowboys T-shirt.

"Cooling off," she said dryly, gesturing in the direction in which he'd gone.

Dani blinked. "Outside? Isn't it hot out there?"

Not half as hot as it had been in the kitchen a few moments before, Kelly thought. "It is," she said, and scooped her daughter up, tickling her until she convulsed with giggles. "That was just an expression."

Dani seemed content with the explanation. She wound her arms around Kelly's neck and delivered several smacking kisses to her face. "I really, really missed you, Mommy."

"Not half as much as I missed you."

Her daughter frowned. "Do you think Jordan missed me?"

"I know he did."

"How do you know?"

"Because he bought you a present every single day," she said, thinking of the pile of stuffed animals and dolls that had accumulated in the room that would be Dani's for however long it took for Jordan to relocate the business.

"Where are they?" Dani demanded, scrambling down.

"Most of them are in your new room in Houston, but I think he did bring one thing back for you. As soon as you eat your breakfast, you can run outside and track him down. I know he's very anxious for you to see it."

Dani headed for the door. "I want to see it now."

Kelly blocked her way. "After you eat and get dressed, young lady." She handed her a glass of orange juice. "Drink this, while I make pancakes."

"Can't I have cereal?" Dani pleaded, bouncing up and down. "It's faster."

"Okay, fine." She poured a bowlful of corn flakes, added milk and slices of banana. "Here you go."

As she spooned up the cereal, Dani tried speculating on what Jordan had brought her. "I'll bet it's a dollhouse," she said, her gaze fixed on Kelly's face.

"I'm not saying," Kelly said, forcing herself to remain expressionless. "It's Jordan's surprise."

"Is it a new teddy bear, a great big one?"

Kelly grinned at her persistence. "I'm not saying," she repeated.

"Please, Mommy, my tummy will get all inside out, if I don't know really, really soon."

"Then you'd better stop asking so many questions and finish that cereal," Kelly advised.

Dani fell silent and concentrated on her breakfast. The instant she'd spooned the last bite into her mouth, she climbed down from her chair and raced for the back door.

"Whoa! Clothes, remember?"

Dani managed to exchange her T-shirt for shorts and a top in record time. She waved as she ran past Kelly. "'Bye, Mommy."

On the other side of the screen door, though, she hesitated. "Mommy?"

"What?"

"Can I call Jordan *Daddy?* I know he said at the wedding that he was my new daddy, but he didn't say what I should call him."

Kelly's heart swelled with emotion at the plaintive request. If only Jordan really were her daddy, she thought with regret. "That's up to you and Jordan. Why don't you discuss it with him?"

"Will my real daddy be mad?"

Kelly doubted Paul Flint would much care one way or the other. Given how seldom he showed his face, it was doubtful he'd ever even know.

"I don't think so, munchkin. I think he'd want you to do whatever makes you happy."

It was a blatant lie, but Kelly would do whatever it took to keep Dani from ever discovering that, at least not until she was old enough to judge her father's behavior for herself. She would have to be the one to put the labels—selfish and uncaring came to mind—on it.

"All right!" Dani enthused. "I can hardly wait to see Jordan. He's the very bestest daddy in the world."

Maybe not the bestest quite yet, Kelly thought, smiling as she watched Dani go racing off in the direction of the barn. But he was working on it. By the time they had a baby of their own—*if* they had a baby of their own, she corrected—she was convinced he'd have it down pat.

First, though, he had to give some serious thought to his motivation for parenthood. Hopefully, he would come back from his walk with all the right words. If he didn't, if his reasons were as muddy as the ones behind his decision to marry her, she resolved that hell would freeze over before she would have his child.

And there would remain this huge empty space inside her, a space meant to be filled by all the love she had to share with Jordan's children.

Jordan heard Dani's shouts long before he spotted her. She was racing down the lane as fast as her churning little legs could carry her. He stooped down and held out his arms. She ran into them and flung her arms around his neck. Why hadn't he ever guessed how being a parent would make him feel?

"I was sleeping when you came to get me last night and I never, ever, woke up until this morning," she said.

"I noticed," he said, loving the way she smelled of bubble bath, loving even more the fierce protectiveness she aroused in him.

"Did you miss me?" she demanded.

"Every single minute," he confirmed. "But I'll bet you didn't miss me and your mom at all."

"Sure I did. I even drew you a picture. Want to see it?"

"Of course, I want to see it," he said as she reached into her pocket and pulled out a piece of paper that had been folded and refolded into a small, rumpled square. Jordan took it and spread it open. Tears sprang to his eyes as he saw what she'd depicted.

There, drawn with the brightest crayons in the box, were Kelly and Dani, standing in front of a lopsided house that was recognizable as this one. He was standing between them. In case the drawing itself wasn't clear, she had labeled each of them in crooked letters—Mommy, Dani and Daddy. A fat black cat— or something that vaguely resembled one—was at their feet. A striped cat was clutched in Dani's arms. Kelly was also holding something.

"What's that?" he asked, though he had a pretty good idea.

"That's my baby sister," she said. "See the pink blanket? That's how you know it's a girl."

Jordan nodded solemnly, since he couldn't seem to squeeze a word past the lump lodged in his throat. Across the top Dani had written in large, tilting letters, My Family.

"Did you show this to your mom?"

"Not yet. I made it for you. Will you hang it in your office?"

"You bet I will," he promised.

"Are we going to have a baby?" Dani asked worriedly. "I really, really want a sister."

Jordan saw an opportunity to probe this pint-size genius's mind for an argument he could offer Kelly on the same topic. "Why?"

"So we can play with our doll's together," she said at once. "I tried with Angela, but she's pretty little. She couldn't even hold the doll."

"Babies generally start out pretty little," he mused.

"Couldn't you and mommy have a big one?"

He chuckled. "I don't think it works that way. So, tell me why else you want a sister?"

Dani's face scrunched up as she gave serious thought to the question. "So we can love her to pieces. Mommy always says she loves me to pieces." She looked up at him. "I think she loves you to pieces, too."

An interesting tidbit of news, Jordan thought. "She does? What makes you think so?" he asked, pushing aside how pitiful it was to be pumping a five-year-old for information on his own wife.

Dani gave him a disgusted look. "Because she married you, silly."

Realistically, Jordan supposed that was one explanation for Kelly's decision, even if she'd never flat-out said it. His spirits rose a fraction. "Anything else?"

"She thinks you're a saint."

Jordan stared. "A saint? What makes you think that?"

"'Cause she always said the only way she'd ever get married again was if a saint came along. And we learned in Sunday school that you should love saints, right?"

He found the logic a little convoluted, but essentially correct. It was certainly a topic worth discussing with his wife.

"Jordan?"

"Yes, munchkin?" he said distractedly, his thoughts already leaping ahead to the conversation he would have with Kelly the instant he got back to the house.

"I been thinking."

"Oh?"

"I think maybe I should call you Daddy," she said, gazing at him soberly. "What do you think?"

He gave her a fierce hug. "I think there's nothing that would make me any happier."

"Really?"

"Really, really," he confirmed. He took her hand. "Why don't we go back to the house and I'll show you what I brought for you?"

"You brought me a present?" Dani asked, looking a little too innocent.

"I did, indeed," he said. And in another nine months or so, he intended to see that another of her dreams came true. She would have that baby sister—or a brother, if nature got the order mixed up.

As they reached his car he paused and opened the trunk, removing a huge box that had taken up every square inch of room. He watched in delight as Dani saw the picture on the side and a grin spread across her face.

"It's a baby buggy," she said. "Hurry, Daddy. Open it up."

The minute he had the small pink carriage out of the box, Dani grabbed the handle and began propelling it straight toward the barn. Jordan stared after her in bemusement.

"Where are you going?" he shouted.

"To get Francie and the kittens. I'm going to take them for a ride."

"It's supposed to be for your dolls."

"But I know that Francie really, really wants to go for a ride."

Jordan had his doubts, but he let her go. He had more important things to settle.

He found Kelly inside doing laundry. She'd changed to a pair of incredibly provocative shorts and a halter top. The dryer had made the laundry room steamy. Her skin glistened with a sheen of dampness. With all of the noise from the washer and dryer, she didn't hear him approaching. He slipped up behind her, wrapped his arms around her waist and sprinkled kisses across her bare shoulders.

"Nice," she murmured, and turned in his loose embrace to claim a real kiss.

Her body fit snugly against his. Heat shot through his veins. On any other occasion the distraction would have worked. Today, though, Jordan had something more than sex on his mind, even though he was relieved by the discovery that she no longer seemed to be quite so furious with him.

"Dani and I have been having quite a chat," he told her.

"Really? How'd she like the carriage?"

"She's out in the barn even as we speak, gathering up Francie and the kittens for a ride."

Kelly grimaced. "I'm sure Francie will love that. Maybe we should go rescue her."

"Francie can take care of herself," he said. "Right now, I want to talk about a picture Dani drew for me." He showed her the folded paper.

"And this is?" Kelly inquired, pointing to the pink bundle in her arms.

"Her baby sister."

Kelly's gaze shot to his. "Did you put her up to this?"

"No, but the picture got me to thinking. The one thing the family in this picture has that we haven't talked about is love."

"Evidenced by all the hearts, I suppose?"

"Exactly." He kept his gaze fixed on Kelly's face and thought he read something that might have been uncertainty in the depths of her eyes. As if he'd been struck by a bolt of lightning, the last piece of the puzzle suddenly came clear. Kelly did love him still, just as she once had and just as Dani had said. She'd just been waiting for him to wake up and discover that he loved her.

"I realized something when I saw this. I do love you," he admitted, finally finding the right words to express all the things he'd been feeling over the past weeks and months. As soon as the words were out, he realized exactly how right they were.

"That's why I want to fill this house with our children," he explained, trying to make her see all that he'd discovered in his heart. "There are so many more reasons, too. Dani shouldn't be an only child. Any child who is a part of you will steal my heart."

He grinned at the transformation he saw on her face. "Am I getting warm?" he asked, even though he could read the answer in her smile.

"I don't know about you, but I'm getting very warm." She searched his face. "Are you sure this is what you want? If we have a child, there's no turning back."

"There was never any chance of turning back," he said with certainty. "To borrow a phrase from your daughter, I love you to pieces." He gave her a lazy smile. "I may be slow, sweet pea, but once I get there, I never, ever, change my mind. Guaranteed."

Epilogue

"I think we should get the whole family together and go into town for dinner tonight," Kelly announced on a Sunday in mid-June, almost ten months after their marriage. "I've already called Jessie. She and Luke will drive over this afternoon. Do you want to call your parents or should I?"

Jordan regarded his wife warily. "You never want to get together with my parents. You always say my mother gives you hives."

"I can tolerate her criticism for one night. And I adore Harlan."

He nodded. "So, what's the occasion? It's not your birthday." She had turned thirty without mishap a few weeks before. "It's not mine. It's not our anniversary."

"You sure about all that?" she taunted.

"I'd like to claim total credit, but believe me, Ginger never lets me forget. She says there are certain things that are inviolate in a good marriage and special occasions top the list. She puts every important date on my calendar and circles it in red."

"A wise woman," Kelly enthused.

"You still haven't said what's going on."

"It's a surprise."

Her reticence was making Jordan extremely nervous. Every once in a while, Kelly devised some scheme that threw the wonderful, quiet routine of their marriage into chaos. He had a hunch this was going to be one of those times. He was still reeling from the discovery that in seeking serenity, he'd found a woman filled with surprises.

"Does Dani know?" he inquired innocently.

Kelly chuckled. "Absolutely not. I know she can't keep a secret, especially from you. Do you bribe that child or what?"

"Never."

"Are you calling your parents or not?"

He sighed. "I'll call them. What time and where?"

"DiPasquali's at seven."

Jordan spent the rest of the day surreptitiously observing his wife and trying to figure out what was going on in her head. The predictability he'd once cherished in Kelly had obviously vanished sometime after puberty without his noticing. She'd become a totally perplexing, complicated—okay, fascinating—

woman. There wasn't a day that passed that he didn't thank his lucky stars that he'd been smart enough to marry her.

When they arrived at the Italian restaurant that night, Gina and Anthony had already pushed several tables together for them in the middle of the room. Jordan had the distinct impression that they, too, were in on this hush-hush secret.

In fact, only the men in the family seemed to be left out. Luke and his father seemed as bemused by all the fuss as he was. The women were all smiling conspiratorially—even his mother—which only added to his nervousness. He was tempted to run out and call Ginger just to make sure a special occasion hadn't slipped his mind, after all.

Kelly seemed inclined to prolong his agony, too. Not a word about what had drawn them together was spoken all during the noisy, laughter-filled dinner. Only after they'd finished the pizza did he glance at the other end of the table where Kelly was seated next to Jessie and her almost-two-year-old daughter, Angela. Kelly was whispering to Gina, who smiled broadly and nodded.

"I will get dessert now," the restaurant owner said.

"Bring me some of that Italian ice cream," Harlan said. "What's it called? Spumoni?"

"Not tonight," Kelly said. "I've arranged for something special."

Jordan's gaze shot to hers. Her expression was unreadable and she refused to meet his eyes.

"Anyone like coffee?" Gina DiPasquali asked.

"Another beer for me," Harlan said.

"I'll take the coffee," Luke told her. He leaned over and kissed Jessie's cheek. "What about you? Coffee?"

Jessie nodded.

As soon as the order was complete, Gina vanished into the kitchen. A moment later she returned, dispensing cups and filling them with coffee. She brought Harlan's beer from the bar, then disappeared again.

A few minutes after that the restaurant lights inexplicably dimmed. Jordan started to get to his feet, but his father stopped him with a firm grasp of his arm and a gesture toward the kitchen. He looked up and saw Gina carrying a cake ablaze with candles. Once again, his heart climbed into his throat. Whose birthday was it? And why the hell hadn't Kelly or Ginger, either one, just told him? He felt like an idiot.

To his complete consternation, Gina seemed to be heading his way. She lowered the cake to the table in front of him.

His startled gaze sought out his wife. "It's not my birthday," he said.

"Read the inscription," she suggested.

He glanced down at the huge white cake with its pink roses and blue writing. Happy Father's Day, Jordan, it read. Love Kelly, Dani And ???

Father's Day? Wasn't that one of the ones Ginger was supposed to remind him about? And shouldn't this cake be for Harlan?

He looked around the table and saw everyone grinning expectantly. *Father's Day?* Question marks? His name, not his father's on the cake? The implication finally sank in. All of the breath whooshed out of him.

His gaze shot up. "Is this ... Are you ..."

Kelly's head bobbed up and down. "We're going to have a baby," she confirmed as the entire table erupted into applause.

Jordan's pulse raced. His eyes locked with his wife's and stayed there as he moved from his chair and headed straight for her. A baby? They were going to have a baby! Suddenly he was afraid his heart might burst from sheer joy.

Kelly stood and hurried into his arms.

"I love you," he whispered against her soft, fragrant hair. "More every single day."

"I love you."

"Me, too, Mommy. Me, too," Dani said, tugging on their shirtsleeves.

Jordan reached down and hefted her into his arms. "You, too, munchkin. We love you, too." He glanced around at the others and a smile spread across his face. "Happy Father's Day, everyone!"

He saw his mother reach for his father's hand and squeeze it. Tears glistened in his father's eyes as he looked from his wife to his two sons and back again. Luke's hand had settled possessively on Angela's tiny shoulder. Jessie rested her hand on top of his. Angela's birth had brought them together. Today they were happier than ever.

During his entire life, Father's Day had been one of those occasions that Jordan acknowledged dutifully but without much thought or emotion. Ginger usually picked out the card and gift for his father, often sending it without even getting his signature. It had happened just that way this year, he was sure.

He doubted that he would ever treat the occasion so cavalierly after today, though. From now on, he knew that being a father would give him the kind of emotional fulfillment he had once despaired of ever feeling. Maybe it was true what Kelly had once said to him, maybe he really was a natural born daddy.

In the midst of their celebration, he happened to glance across the restaurant. Melissa Horton was sitting in a booth all alone, her expression forlorn as she watched the family she had once wanted so badly to be a part of. Even across the room, he could detect the tears shimmering in her eyes.

Jordan was about to go and ask her to join them when she hurriedly stood, then bent over to retrieve something from the booth. To his astonishment, he saw that it was a baby carrier.

Stunned, he was drawn across the room despite himself. Perhaps he was thinking of the news he'd just received. Perhaps he was thinking of his brother, settled now on a ranch in Wyoming and determined never to set foot in Texas again because of this woman.

"Melissa," Jordan acknowledged, stopping her in her tracks with the quiet command in his voice.

She blinked hard, fighting those unmistakable tears, then finally faced him, her chin tilted defiantly. "Hello, Jordan."

He automatically glanced at her hand, wondering why he'd never heard that she had married. It would have been the kind of news that his family would surely have been aware of. Her ring finger was bare.

He turned his attention to the carrier. "May I see? I just found out that I'm going to be a father in a few months. When I saw you had a baby, I couldn't resist."

She looked as if she'd rather sink straight through the floor, but she eventually nodded and put the carrier onto the table. By this time Kelly had wandered over to join him, tucking her hand into his.

"She's darling," Kelly said when Jordan stood there in stunned silence, unable to form a single word.

He didn't know much about babies. He'd heard they all looked the same, but he was absolutely certain that the infant with the huge brown eyes and dark tuft of hair looked exactly like an Adams. Except for the pink bow tied around the hair, she was a dead ringer for pictures he'd seen of Cody, chubby little cheeks and all.

Alarm darkened Melissa's eyes as she watched his reaction.

"She's Cody's, isn't she?" he said more harshly than he'd intended. Kelly stared at him in shock, then looked again at the baby.

Tears spilled down Melissa's cheeks. "Don't tell him. Please. He'll just hate me. Promise you won't tell him."

Jordan couldn't make any such promise. Nor, from the expression he saw in Kelly's eyes, was she willing to guarantee her silence, either.

"Not without talking to you," Kelly said quietly, giving the young woman a hug. "I'll be in touch."

Apparently satisfied with the answer, Melissa picked up her baby and fled.

"We have to tell him," Jordan said, keeping his voice hushed so the others wouldn't hear. Harlan would have a fit, if he ever found out.

He glanced back toward the table, where no one else seemed to have taken much notice of the exchange. They'd all taken Cody's side against Melissa and obviously considered her presence here tonight not worthy of their attention. "What do we tell them?"

"Nothing until we've had a chance to think about all of the ramifications," Kelly said sensibly. "Now let's go back to the others and celebrate our news, okay? I don't want anything spoiling this moment."

Jordan forced his anxieties about his brother and this baby Cody knew nothing about from his mind. He leaned down and kissed his wife. Whatever they decided to do about Melissa and Cody, they would decide it together.

"I love you," he said again, thinking how incredibly lucky he was. "Love me?"

"Always." She touched her hand to his cheek and met his eyes. "Always."

* * * * *

Be sure to watch for
THE COWBOY AND HIS BABY to find out
what Cody decides to do when he discovers
that he has a daughter with the woman he
vowed never to see again.
Coming in February 1996
from Silhouette Special Edition.

Dear Reader,

The celebration of Silhouette Special Edition's one thousandth book goes on, proving that there are always more wonderful stories of love, laughter and passion to be told.

I am so proud to be among the authors in this special imprint of Silhouette Books. When I wrote my first Special Edition, *Safe Harbor,* back in 1987, I was joining a tradition that had already been in place for more than four hundred books.

After writing only the shorter contemporary romances, there was some question in my mind about whether I had enough to say to satisfy the longer length. What I quickly discovered was that Special Edition gave me the space to explore relationships in more depth, to tell richer, more emotional stories. I was able to surround my characters with friends and relatives to create whole communities, much like the communities in which each of us lives.

I hope you're enjoying the world of Harlan Adams and his three sons in the And Baby Makes Three quartet of books. So far, you've already read about Luke and Jordan. Next time in *The Cowboy and His Baby,* you'll spend time with Cody as he fights for his child...and the woman he's always loved. And then it's Daddy's turn, when Harlan Adams's fate takes a most unusual twist in *The Rancher and His Unexpected Daughter.*

I also hope you'll go on enjoying Silhouette Special Edition for years to come. It's a very special tradition in romance.

Sherryl Woods

Silhouette®

SPECIAL EDITION™

COMING NEXT MONTH

Take 4 bestselling love stories FREE

Plus get a FREE surprise gift!

Special Limited-time Offer

Mail to Silhouette Reader Service™

3010 Walden Avenue
P.O. Box 1867
Buffalo, N.Y. 14269-1867

YES! Please send me 4 free Silhouette Special Edition® novels and my free surprise gift. Then send me 6 brand-new novels every month, which I will receive months before they appear in bookstores. Bill me at the low price of $3.12 each plus 25¢ delivery and applicable sales tax, if any.* That's the complete price and a savings of over 10% off the cover prices—quite a bargain! I understand that accepting the books and gift places me under no obligation ever to buy any books. I can always return a shipment and cancel at any time. Even if I never buy another book from Silhouette, the 4 free books and the surprise gift are mine to keep forever.

235 BPA AW6Y

Name	(PLEASE PRINT)	
Address	Apt. No.	
City	State	Zip

This offer is limited to one order per household and not valid to present Silhouette Special Edition® subscribers. *Terms and prices are subject to change without notice. Sales tax applicable in N.Y.

USPED-995

©1990 Harlequin Enterprises Limited

SILHOUETTE®

Desire®

CELEBRATION 1000

is on its way
in April, May and June 1996!

Join us for the celebration of Desire's 1000th book!
We'll have

- Book #1000, *Man of Ice* by Diana Palmer in May!
- Best-loved miniseries such as **Hawk's Way** by Joan Johnston, and **Daughters of Texas** by Annette Broadrick
- Fabulous new writers in our Debut author program, where you can collect <u>double</u> Pages and Privileges Proofs of Purchase

Plus you can enter our exciting Sweepstakes for a chance to win a beautiful piece of original Silhouette Desire cover art or one of many autographed Silhouette Desire books!

SILHOUETTE DESIRE'S CELEBRATION 1000
...because the best is yet to come!

Bestselling author

RACHEL LEE

takes her Conard County series to new heights with

A CONARD COUNTY Reckoning

This March, Rachel Lee brings readers a brand-new, longer-length, out-of-series title featuring the characters from her successful Conard County miniseries.

Janet Tate and Abel Pierce have both been betrayed and carry deep, bitter memories. Brought together by great passion, they must learn to trust again.

"Conard County is a wonderful place to visit! Rachel Lee has crafted warm, enchanting stories. These are wonderful books to curl up with and read. I highly recommend them."
—*New York Times* bestselling author
Heather Graham Pozzessere

Available in March, wherever Silhouette books are sold.

You're About to Become a Privileged Woman

Privileged Woman

Reap the rewards of fabulous free gifts and benefits with proofs-of-purchase from Silhouette and Harlequin books

Pages & Privileges™

It's our way of thanking you for buying our books at your favorite retail stores.

PROOF OF PURCHASE
SSE-PP98
Offer expires October 31, 1996

BONUS
Proof of Purchase
BSSE-PP94
Offer expires October 31, 1996

Harlequin and Silhouette—
the most privileged readers in the world!

For more information about Harlequin and Silhouette's PAGES & PRIVILEGES program call the Pages & Privileges Benefits Desk: **1-503-794-2499**